Bulwick School

A Yankee Lad in London

Robert A. Lytle

BRIGHTON PUBLISHING LLC
435 N. HARRIS DRIVE
MESA, AZ 85203

BULWICK SCHOOL
A YANKEE LAD IN LONDON

ROBERT A. LYTLE

BRIGHTON PUBLISHING LLC
435 N. HARRIS DRIVE
MESA, AZ 85203
WWW.BRIGHTONPUBLISHING.COM

COPYRIGHT © 2013

ISBN 13: 978-1-621831-54-9
ISBN 10: 1-62183-154-X

PRINTED IN THE UNITED STATES OF AMERICA

FIRST EDITION

COVER DESIGN: TOM RODRIGUEZ

Acknowledgements

~~~

T hrough my writing, revising, and research I have asked for, and received help, from many.

These are but a few:

Ken Johnson
Javan Kienzle
John Mohr
Mary and Jack Irvine
Hugh Thompson
Bob and Gaynor Scruton
Anthony Tocco
Cindy Barnwell
Marilyn Anderson
Mike Norris
Candi Schwark
Jeffrey T. Frazier

Prologue

Picture this...

SLAM*!*

That's me crashing into a wall of lockers. Pain shoots through my right hip and shoulder.

RAGE*!*

That's me saying, "What was that?" My head is spinning. In a blur, I see dozens of kids in the hall. They're all staring. It's the middle of November—my first day at North Middle.

B-r-r-r-ing-g-g!

That's the bell.

Everyone disappears into classrooms. I'm sitting there, holding a sheet of paper. I glance up. My eyes focus on this huge, no-neck bozo. He hovers over me—his ugly face inches from mine.

"Watch where you're goin,' Butthead," he says and turns away.

I'm alone, and not for the last time.

Chapter One

~~~~

This story is about bullying. Bullying has many names. When you're little—say, three or four years old, your older brothers or sisters call you Twerp or Squirt. That's teasing. It makes you mad, but that's why they do it—to get your goat. It doesn't hurt, I mean, physically. You tell your mom. She scolds them, but that's about it.

You turn five and go to school. On the bus bigger kids push you around, twist your arm or punch you. It shows their pals how tough they are, that they have control over someone—even if it's someone smaller than they are. That's the kind of bullying most people think of when they hear the word. But that's not the worst kind of bullying. It's not even close.

Next, you're in middle school. You get in a club, join the band or make a team sport. The older members make you do their grunt work. You carry their bags and polish their shoes. That's hazing. You don't like it, but it's mostly in good fun, like being initiated into a club. Still, you tell yourself that you won't do that when you're in their place. You'll be a bigger person than that. You shake it off and bide your time.

Now, you're in high school. You're texting your friends when, out of nowhere, a really nasty message appears on your phone—some totally false, horrible thing about you. You have no idea where it came from, but there it is. Everyone can read it. Everyone *does* read it. You have no way to stop it, even if you know who's doing it. You get physically ill. Your friends quit sitting with you at lunch. They're afraid they'll be the next victims. That's cyber-bullying. It's mean spirited and the torture is intended. That really hurts.

And then you get a job. Even if it's just an after-school one, bagging groceries. One of the older employees—another bagger, a cashier, even the manager—starts picking on you. You stand up for yourself. Things go south as the person keeps it up. The money isn't worth it, but if you quit and try to get another job, your boss will give you a bad recommendation. That's harassment.

There are lots of other words for bullying: prejudice, bigotry, intolerance, discrimination, but they all amount to dividing people and controlling them.

All these things are bad, but they're nothing compared to what's next.

The very worst kind of bullying is terrorism.

Terrorism is when maniacs use car bombs, jet planes and anything they can think of to threaten whole countries. Terrorists kill thousands of people: your family, your friends. The whole world lives in constant fear of their next attack.

This is my story. This is what happened to me.

I survived 9/11, the single worst day of terrorism in the history of the world.

My parents did not.

My name is Michael Hanlon. I was thirteen—almost fourteen—a ninth-grader at Madison High. I was living at home with my mom and dad in the little town of Eastham, New York, which is about thirty miles outside New York City. It was Tuesday, just a regular September morning. I was going to my first-hour English class for a quiz.

I was a bit on edge because English is my worst subject. I'm okay with math and science and most of the others because they have rules, and the rules stay the same no matter what teacher you have. But English? For every spelling, punctuation and grammar rule, there about a dozen exceptions. And it seems like every teacher uses different ones to grade you. English is impossible.

Anyway, in the week I'd been at Madison High, life was looking pretty good, I mean, except for first hour—you know, English. There were a bunch of cool girls, some from my old middle school and some from two other schools that funneled into Madison High. Also, it looked like I'd be playing quarterback for the JV football team, not like I'm any great jock, but I was good enough to play. I only tell you this because it's important later on.

Another nice thing about the start of ninth grade was that most of my buddies, the Counts, were in my lunch period. I should tell you who the Counts were. We were just regular guys, no special jackets, no secret handshakes, nothing like that. We'd get together once a week, Fridays usually, for dinner. Some moms went all out and put on fancy spreads. Others just ordered in pizza. It didn't matter to us what we ate. What was important was that we could get together, go to a movie or a ball game, and they'd know where we were. They wouldn't get all stressed out wondering what we were doing.

Okay, back to the English class. It was on that Tuesday morning as I was walking to my desk that I remember thinking about the year before when we had just moved to Eastham.

My father was Brendan—he was named for an Irish poet. And my mom, Anne—she was named for some English queen or princess. Anyway, they had decided to move from our old place in Brooklyn to Eastham. It was in November and for me, the timing was awful. When I got to my new school it was already two months into the first marking period. On the very first day, I had to get my locker, find my classrooms and sort everything out for myself.

By then everyone was in his own group—jocks, greasers, nerds, preppies—whatever. And if you weren't in, you were out. As a new kid, I was definitely out. I walked through the halls that morning feeling like a mouse in a snake pit. Everyone was looking at me like, who is that?

Right away, this big, no-neck bozo hip-checks me into a wall of lockers. He glares at me like I had no business coming within three feet of him. He pushes his chin into my face and tells me to watch where I'm going.

I didn't know it then, but I found out later that his name was Joey Cardle. He was the chief goon in a gang of other bottom feeders. His leather jacket read "Demons."

Like I said, I grew up in Brooklyn, so I pretty much knew trouble when I saw it. And this guy was trouble.

Just then the bell rang. I slipped past him and ducked into class.

During the period, what with finding a desk, signing out a textbook, and trying to take notes, I forgot all about Joey. But when the bell rang and I left the room, there he was. This time he was with three of his lowlife pals, all in their leather jackets. Again, he got in my face, nodded at me and said to his buds, "This is the kid we're gonna do."

Six classes later the last bell rang and I went to my locker. I grabbed my book bag and met up with Andy Lang, the kid I'd met the day before and who lived next door to my new house. We started walking home and, along the way, Andy told me stuff about the street—what yards I could cut through and which ones I'd get yelled at if I tried, things like that. All the while I kept thinking about Joey's threat.

Since I'd grown up in Brooklyn, Eastham seemed pretty tame. Actually, that's why my parents had moved there. My new street, the neighborhood, the whole town was like a sleepy little burb. As Andy and I got close to my street I started feeling better, like maybe Joey was just spouting off to his buddies and nothing was going to come of it. We turned the corner and Andy started telling me about one kid that I'd better not get on the wrong side of. He said the boy's name was Joey Cardle, and he lived in this huge house we were about to pass.

"People say Joey's dad is a mob boss," Andy said. "Joey and his Demons pals are sort of like his father's minor league thugs—ready, willing and able to move up to the big time. He's beat me bloody so many times I've given up count."

We walked past the enormous gate. Just then four guys jumped out from behind it. One was the boy I'd seen in the hall. This time I noticed "Joey" was stitched into his leather jacket. His eyes seemed bigger than baseballs—like he was on some sort of upper. He shoved Andy to the ground and said to me, "Hey, Butthead, you wanna go down my street? You gotta go through me."

They had me surrounded. My only chance was to make a break for it. I looked for the weakest link, but each guy had me by about thirty pounds. I turned and faced Joey. "Look," I said, "you got me mixed up with someone else." I glanced down at the ground. Andy was staring up at Joey. Andy's face was as white as a roll of Charmin.

"Please, Joey," Andy cried. "Let me go. I won't tell."

Joey snorted. He nodded to his pals. Just like that, they let Andy out of the circle. He vanished in a heartbeat.

Before I could move, the three guys closed the circle. It was just me and Joey. His upper lip curled into a sneer. He growled, "No, Stupid, I mean you."

"Get 'im, Joey," one of his buddies said.

Joey grabbed my head. He yanked me into his armpit and began to squeeze my brains out. His breath could have stopped a clock. With a desperate jerk I slipped out of his grip.

I turned to run, but he grabbed my jacket, ripping the sleeve. He spun me around and threw me to the ground.

Out of the corner of my eye I saw him raring back with his right foot. He was about to send a boot into my ribs. I rolled away and scrambled to my feet. Again, he was in my face, but this time he was unloading a brass-knuckle-enhanced, right hook. He aimed it for my left ear and let fly. I ducked and heard his fist whistle over my head.

He stumbled, off balance from his missed swing.

In that split-second I got my only chance of getting away alive. I clenched my right fist and launched an uppercut. I gave it everything I had. It met his chin with a shattering crunch.

I've been in fights before, but I'd never hit anybody so hard in all my life, not even in the self-defense class I'd taken at the Brooklyn Y. There, we'd fought using those overstuffed boxing gloves that are bigger than catchers' mitts. The guys in the class, even the instructors, wore helmets that could smother a neutron bomb.

I knew right away I'd broken his jaw.

Joey straightened in his tracks and stared dumbly at me. Then his eyes rolled back, his knees buckled and he slumped to the ground like a sack of laundry. He stayed there, stock still, except his legs twitched like you see squirrels do when they've just been run over by a truck.

"You killed him," one of his buddies said. We all stood there. Nobody moved.

Then, from a distance, I heard a siren. It kept getting louder until suddenly, it stopped. I turned and saw two cops running toward us. The first one bent over Joey. The second one pulled out a club. "Who did this?" he barked. Joey's pals all pointed at me.

The first cop squared himself in my face. "Gimme some ID," he ordered. I fumbled around in my back pocket for my school card and handed it to him.

One cop said to the other, "Call an ambulance. It's Joey Cardle. Better phone his dad, too. He'll want to know who did this to his boy."

I was in big trouble. If the cops were on a first name basis with the mob boss's son, what chance did I have? All I could hope for was that Joey's dad would find out his son had started the fight and would drop the whole thing. Wishful thinking.

In minutes, another siren screeched to a stop. Joey was loaded into an ambulance and sent on his way. The second policeman let Joey's pals go without even getting their names, like he already knew who they were. Then he pushed me into the back seat of the cop car. He said he wanted to see my parents. He asked me where I lived. I said my house was just up the street, but that my mom and dad were still at work.

He said, "We'll check that out. Right now, we're taking you home. Get inside and stay put."

When we got to my house I unlocked the front door. I went in, washed up and changed clothes.

Half an hour later I heard the garage door opening. I looked into the driveway and saw our blue Taurus. My parents were home. Dad dropped Mom off at the side door and then parked the car. Mom came in and I yelled, "Hi," down from my bedroom, like nothing was wrong. But as she walked by the laundry room she must have seen my dirty clothes.

She called me downstairs. When I got there, she was wiggling her finger through the rip in my jacket. It didn't take her long to get the whole story out of me.

Just when I had almost talked her into thinking it was no big deal, Dad came in. I had to go over it all with him. A few minutes later the phone rang.

Chapter Two

On the second ring Dad answered it. I guessed right away that it was Joey's father. I could hear only my dad's end of the conversation, but I figured out pretty quick that it wasn't going well. I could tell Dad was upset because he started talking in his old Irish brogue. A long time ago Mom and Dad both had really strong accents, but each worked hard to drop them. Dad said a foreign accent made people think you'd just fallen off the boat.

If you were a salesman, like Dad was, your customers wouldn't take any stock in what you had to say. Mom said the same about her job, which was executive secretary in a big telecommunications firm. Actually, Mom sounded more like she was from England—like the Queen or someone—even though Mom and Dad both came from the same town in Ireland.

Anyway, the longer Dad was on the phone the stronger his old accent got, so I knew something really bad was going on. I found out that Joey would live, but I might go to jail. Dad repeated the words "aggravated assault" and "attempted murder" a couple of times.

Dad hung up and turned to me with a worried look. "D' yeh know who this Mr. Cardle is?" he asked.

"Just what I told you, mob boss maybe," I said. "His son's a total jerk."

"Aye, that he may be," Dad said, "but you struck him, so you did—busted his jaw, gave him a concussion. He might have died. Mr. Cardle says if you own up to starting the fight, he'll have the charges dropped to simple assault."

"But I didn't start it," I said. "Why should I say I did? Joey'd been getting in my face at school all day. I was almost home when he and his pals cornered us. Joey might have killed me if I hadn't gotten in one lucky punch. Ask Andy Lang. He was with me—at least for a while. There were four of them. They jumped me."

"Joey's mates say otherwise," Dad said. "They say you had it in for him. They say they came along just as you were beating Joey's brains out. Mr. Cardle says it's in the police report. And the report says nothing about Andy Lang. Mr. Cardle is suing for damages. He says if you don't admit to starting it, he'll do more than sue. He'll have you tried as an adult, so he says. They'll toss you in jail and throw away the key."

"That's crazy," I said. "I was just standing up for myself. I didn't start anything."

"Aye," he said, "but whether you did or didn't doesn't matter to a judge—not if you don't have someone to back you up. It was your blow that finished it."

"Dad, it was self-defense. I tried to get away. You have to believe me."

He stared straight at me for a long time. Then his expression softened and he put his hand on my shoulder. "All right, Michael, I believe you," he said. "And if I'm not mistaken, our mobster friend knows it, too. And he knows that if he can make you say you started it, it will put you on the hook and let his son off of it. I've seen this before back in Ireland. When a bloke like him gets a hold over you, he'll have you in his power forever. Michael, I'm not going to let that happen. I have a feeling Mr. Cardle may not be ready for this, but we're going to stand up to him."

That night I had my first really bad dream ever. Up until then, if I did dream, it would be fun stuff, like jumping over things—small things at first—people, and then houses. Pretty soon I'd be flying over the Brooklyn Bridge and the Twin Towers.

When I got up in the morning, by the time I dressed, I'd have forgotten about it.

But that night was different. I dreamed I was standing in the middle of a field. Along came a seven-foot-tall, three-hundred-pound goon with a face like Joey Cardle. I turned to get away, but then there was another, then another, until about a hundred Joey Cardles had me boxed in. Suddenly, I wasn't in an open field anymore. I was in one of those wrestling cages like you see on TV. I couldn't move or even breathe. I twisted and turned to get away. The next thing I knew, I'd fallen out of bed and hit my head on the floor. I woke up, not even knowing where I was.

I knew this wouldn't be like the flying dreams. I'd remember this one. And I was right. I couldn't get it out of my head. What was worse, I had the same dream every night for months.

As if that wasn't bad enough, the principal at North Middle made me go to these stupid "anger management" classes. It was his rule that any student caught fighting had to go to them. If I skipped even one session, I'd be kicked out of school. They were held every Wednesday night in the basement of the Eastham Police Department. Kids of all ages, races and sizes were there. The room was right next to the jail cells, which we had to pass to get to the door. As we walked along, the jailbirds taunted us, calling us names and telling us what they'd do if we got put in a cell with them. They might have been the ones on the wrong side of the bars, but it was us who felt the heat. If the principal's idea was to scare us out of our gourds, it worked—at least, for me.

After that was over, my real court case started—the one with a whole gang of Cardle lawyers out to prove that I had tried to kill Joey. That's when it got really scary. Every day my parents and I had to sit in the courtroom while Joey lied his head off in front of the jury. He wore one of those collars like he had a broken neck or something. What a fraud.

And my father was right. The legal fees were putting us in

a real hole. Each of my parents had decent jobs and made pretty good money, but it was nothing compared to what Joey's dad could shell out to protect his sweet little son's honor. Winning the case wasn't enough. Mr. Cardle wanted to crush us—stomp us into the ground and send us packing.

One night I heard Mom ask Dad how much our house could fetch and where we would live if we had to sell. I thought for sure that's what we were going to do—sell out, I mean.

Then, one day, an old woman came to court. She told the judge that she lived across the street from where the fight happened. She'd been sitting on her screened-in porch that day and seen it all. She'd known for years that Joey had been a major troublemaker in the neighborhood, but she also knew what a big shot Mr. Cardle was. She was scared of him and didn't want to get mixed up in the whole thing. When I hit Joey and he went down she said she was glad someone had finally gotten him. But then she saw that Joey wasn't moving, so she called 911.

She watched the cops come and the ambulance haul Joey away. She thought that would be the end of it, but a month later a neighbor lady told her about the court case. She found out that I was the one on trial, not Joey, and that I would go to prison. She decided she couldn't live with herself if she didn't tell the judge what she'd seen, which was exactly what I'd been saying all along.

Hour after hour, Cardle's lawyers grilled her with questions like, "You were fifty or sixty yards from where Mr. Hanlon attacked Mr. Cardle. You were sitting on a screened-in porch and the sky was overcast, so how could you be sure of what you saw?"

They brought in eye doctors and dug up her medical records. They found out she'd had a hip operation and was taking Vicodin. A doctor came in. He told the jury how pain medications can make a person loopy. Then the lawyers asked the lady if she knew how many pills she'd taken that day. When she said she wasn't sure, man, they pounced all over that. They wanted the judge to toss out everything she'd said. The judge said he wouldn't hear of it. He allowed all of what she had said to stay on the record. If he hadn't, I'd have been toast, for sure.

For two days Cardle's lawyers did everything they could to blow holes in her story. They told her if she kept lying, she'd get tossed in jail, too. That just made her mad.

She saw what she saw, and that was that.

Finally, the judge decided he'd seen enough of the lawyers' bullying tactics. He called for the jury's vote. After about five minutes they came out and told the judge that I wasn't guilty. The judge hit his gavel.

The whole thing was over. Joey looked at his dad. Something had changed. Joey had lied to his father, and the mob boss didn't like it.

When I think back on it, I owe a lot to that woman. She put her life on the line—standing up to the Cardles like she did. Without her, I'd have gone to Juvie for sure and then been on probation the rest of my life.

Even though I got off, my parents were still out a ton of money, with all the lost time from work and everything. At least the bleeding was stopped and we kept our house. By the time it was over, Mom wanted to move out of Eastham. Dad shook his head and said he wasn't going to give Mr. Cardle the satisfaction of thinking he had run us out of town. Dad reminded Mom that they had been run off before. He swore then he wouldn't let it happen again. Mom nodded. At the time, I didn't know what they were talking about—being run off before—but now I do.

I also found out that Joey and his buddies had been breaking in new homes—houses that were being built but not yet finished. Joey'd sneak in and pour cans of paint over walls and floors, down the stairs, everywhere.

Joey also got a big kick out of cherry bombing mailboxes. He took great pleasure in kicking spokes out of little kids' bike wheels. He'd been doing all that and a whole bunch of other stuff since he was about eight, but usually nobody caught him at it. If someone did, his dad would put his thug pals on the person's doorstep and scare him into dropping the charge.

Anyway, right after the court case, Mr. Cardle took Joey out of North Middle and put him into a military school in Massachusetts. I thought about Joey a lot, but I sure didn't miss him. Also, after about a month I quit having my cage wrestling dreams.

And I did learn some lessons from the whole thing. If you hit a guy, even in self-defense, you can still go to jail. Dad told me another thing. He said, "Don't take any favors from people if you don't have to—like when Mr. Cardle tried to bluff us into saying you started the fight. Once you're caught in a spider's web, one day you'll be its dinner. He'll eat you bit by bit until there's nothing left of you but an empty shell."

Through all this, I stayed at North Middle; but even with Joey gone, the Demons kept hassling me. They'd trip me in the hall, punch me from behind, stuff like that. They'd do it in open places where, if I fought back, I'd get taken to the principal. With my record, I'd get detention for sure or even expelled.

Finally, early in December, tryouts for North Middle's eighth-grade basketball team began. I showed up, not so much because I was any good, but more to dodge the Demons. My plan was, if Mom and Dad picked me up from practice on their way from work, I wouldn't have to walk home alone. I figured, by the time the coach made his final cuts, the Demons, not known for having terrific attention spans, would have forgotten all about me.

After two weeks the coach posted the roster. My name was on the list. I don't know what he saw in me, because I didn't shoot very well and my ball handling wasn't all that great, but anyway, I made the squad. So, after that, I had a safe way home for the next three months.

One other good thing: Several really great guys were on the team with me. By December, I joined the Counts, the guys I told you about before. As long as I hung around with them, the Demons left me alone. The Counts didn't ask much of me, either. One of their guys moved away, so they needed someone to keep up the ranks. I guess twelve was a good number for them, so I became the new twelfth. From then on, the rest of my year at North Middle went pretty smooth.

Also, one of the Counts, a kid by the name of Roger Byron, taught me how to play guitar. Actually, my Uncle Sean had shown me some chords on a small trail guitar my dad kept under his bed. When I first started playing, I pictured myself in a rock band—playing Beatles or something. But when I fell in with Roger, he taught me all sorts of folk songs instead. He was really into folk music. Up until then, I didn't think anyone was into folk music, not anyone my age, at least.

During lunch period, our school held an open mike at one end of the cafeteria. It was like a mini-version of American Idol. Anyone could play if they wanted to, and it drew quite a crowd. I guess the idea was to keep kids from wandering off the school grounds and getting into mischief. Anyway, Roger sang these really old songs. He was one of those guys that everybody just naturally likes—you know the kind—smart, clever, funny. Anyway, he'd tell the story about some old song and then he'd sing it. He had everyone, teachers even, hanging on his every word. He didn't do anything fancy on his guitar—just simple strumming—but it was the awesome tunes and the amazing stories that kept everyone's attention.

One day I asked him how he'd gotten into it—folk music, I mean.

"Brianna, my girlfriend," he said. "I don't know what started her, but I saw her onstage once. She knocked me out, man. Right then I knew I'd do anything to be with her—even if it took learning how to play guitar, which I had no idea at the time I could do. She told me that all her songs were real stories about real people, not like the pop music you hear on the radio, which is about fake stuff just to sell CDs."

14

Every one of Roger's songs told a different story. Some were English sea chanteys from the 1700s or Irish work songs from the 1800s. Some were about America's problems—war, civil rights—stuff like that.

Pretty soon, I was sitting in with Brianna and Roger, and the three of us were getting pretty good. Life could not be better.

Sometimes, I think about that—how nice it was, because I soon found out that it wouldn't last forever.

Chapter Three

At home, Uncle Sean, my dad's younger brother, was staying with us. He visited our place for about two weeks every year for as long as I can remember. Like my mother and father, Uncle Sean was born in Ireland, but about the time my parents came to America, he moved to England. It's funny, now that I think of it, I never asked Mom and Dad why they came to New York and Uncle Sean landed in London–or why they'd left Ireland in the first place. Maybe kids don't think about those things. I sure didn't. I also never wondered about Uncle's accent. He sounded just like Dad when Dad got upset about something. Dad would stop talking like that as soon as he got control of himself, but Uncle Sean didn't seem to mind sounding Irish at all. In fact, it seemed he'd sprinkle in more of his Irish sayings the longer people listened.

Uncle's stays were always action-packed, but not always fun-filled. Like I said, Dad kept a guitar under his bed. I never saw him use it, but Uncle Sean would haul it out and play for hours. He'd sing songs I never heard anywhere else. They were all about Ireland, but not the sappy Broadway tunes you hear around Saint Patrick's Day–"Galway Bay," "Irish Lullaby" and the like. Instead, his songs were about people getting hanged for fighting Ireland's enemy, which, I found out was England. There was a lot of hatred in those songs–a lot of people dying for the "Cause," whatever that was.

When Uncle Sean and I were home alone he'd tell me how he and Dad were in this secret group, the I.R.A., the Irish Republican Army. He told me how they were going to make Ireland whole again–kick the bloody English out of Northern

16

Ireland—ship the whole lot of 'em back to England where they belonged. Then, all of Ireland would be free, like it should be, run by real Irishmen.

Sometimes, after my parents had gotten home from work and Uncle Sean had downed a few beers, he'd get a little loud, especially for Mom. She could stand his ranting up to a point, but you could tell it got under her skin sometimes. That's when the "action-packed" part became not so "fun-filled." There was a real wall there between Mom and Uncle Sean that I couldn't figure out, at least not then. You'd think since they were both from the "auld sod," as Uncle Sean called Ireland, that they'd get along better. They even came from the same town, a place in Northern Ireland called Belfast.

It finally came out during Uncle's last stay with us that he was in New York to drum up money for the Cause–for his IRA pals back in England. He was the main speaker at the Irish/American Club in the City, and after his speech, someone dropped him off at our house. I was already home from school when he came in. He had a six-pack of Guinness in one hand and a bottle of booze in the other. He made short work of the beers before uncorking the Bushmills, which is Irish whiskey. By the time my parents got home from work, he was pretty much wasted.

That night he yelled at my dad, told him that the true patriots back home needed money–that they couldn't get their freedom from the bloody English without guns, and they couldn't get guns without money. It wasn't like the old days when suitcases full of American cash poured back from Irish emigrants whose families were still struggling under John Bull's tyranny back in the old country. I had no idea who John Bull was, but I found out later that it was Irish slang for the British government.

Uncle Sean was more than a little smashed. He yelled, "How could you forget your roots? Have you forgotten what they did to your mum back in Belfast–how they murdered your da, your two sisters and baby brother?" He was screaming.

My father quietly told Uncle Sean that the Troubles were over. It was 2001 now, not 1973. There was peace, even in Belfast. Guns were the last things the Irish people needed. Besides, Dad said, he had lost more in the name of the Cause than anyone had any right to expect. He would give no more.

I was up in my room when Uncle Sean shouted something about the bloody Prods. A second later the front door slammed. I looked out my window and saw Mom stalk out of the house. She hadn't said a word, but I could tell she was furious.

Dad then told Uncle Sean that when he and Anne left Ireland, it was forever. He told Uncle Sean that he could stay at our house as often as he liked, but he would never give one penny to the Cause. And that was final.

Well, it wasn't final. It was only the beginning.

I told you about Joey Cardle and Uncle Sean for a reason—sort of as background. The real story started on that September morning in ninth grade at Madison High. I was sitting at my desk, doing some last minute cramming for the English quiz, when the bell rang. Mr. Adams closed the door.

Every day, the first few minutes of school were used for announcements. Mr. Adams clicked on the large TV over his head, and a really hot sophomore babe showed up on the screen. She started "The Pledge of Allegiance," and we all stood up. Then we sat down and the camera focused on a serious-looking kid who read the day's messages. Just after he said, "And back to you, Kendra," the picture went garbled. I was still scribbling, "Kendra," into my notebook when, a second later, Principal Brock's face appeared on the screen.

He was smiling and staring into the camera. He said, "Good day, students. This morning, as you were coming to school, an accident occurred that is being covered by all the networks. It is my belief that history takes place around us every day. What has happened only thirty miles away may affect us all. I would be remiss if I didn't use the technology available to allow you to watch its coverage. We will now patch the school monitor into the television broadcast so that you can follow the news story. Until further notice, even though the class bells ring, please remain in your seats. We will resume our regular schedule when the newscast is over."

I glanced over to Gabe Wrobel, one of my Count buddies, sitting in the desk to my left. "All right," I whispered. "We won't have to worry about that quiz."

He nodded and smiled back.

Then the monitor went from Mr. Brock's face to a very familiar sight. There was no sound, but the camera showed the Twin Towers of the World Trade Center.

I knew right away what it was because both my mother and father worked there. Mom was a secretary with TelCor in the North Tower. Dad was a sales manager at Herbert Wilson Advertising in the South Tower. Both had their offices nearly at the top of each building.

I always thought how cool it was that their jobs were so close to each other that they could go to work together. Most of the kids I knew had parents that worked nowhere near each other and had to drive two cars every day. Mom and Dad took turns driving, and it worked out great.

Even now, I can close my eyes and remember this next part word for word. With my first look at the screen I could see that something was horribly wrong. Smoke was pouring out from near the top of one of the buildings. I reminded myself how casually Mr. Brock had mentioned the interruption in our regular school day, like it was no big deal. I figured, okay, a fire had started during the night when the place was empty. It had gotten out of control and would be put out soon, something like that. I wondered: Is it the North Tower where Mom works or the South Tower where Dad has his office? As the camera backed away and showed the rest of Manhattan, I saw that the smoking building was the North Tower, Mom's building. Mom and Dad probably had seen the smoke on their way to work and not even parked their car.

I couldn't tell which floors were smoking, but I could see that it was pretty high up, probably not her floor though.

I knew they both started work at 8:30. I looked at the clock above Mr. Adams' head. It read 9:01. At worst, Mom and Dad would have been stopped in the garage and not even gone up the elevator.

I looked back at the screen. The next thing I saw was totally unreal. With Mom's building already billowing with smoke, a jumbo jet cut across the sky, heading directly for Dad's building. A split second later, like in some horrible video game, the plane sliced into the middle of the South Tower. It exploded into an enormous ball of flames and tore through the building, blasting out through the other side.

At first, I thought it might just be a replay of the first fire. Then the camera backed away and showed both towers in flames.

I stared at the TV, but again told myself that Mom and Dad were safe. It was just recorded film, like it had all happened during the night or way earlier in the morning. The bell rang for the class to change, but nobody moved. There was not another sound in the room. Then, along with the picture, an announcer began to speak.

It was a familiar voice, Tom Brokaw maybe, saying that this second explosion could not have been an accident. He said it looked like the work of Middle East terrorists. Another voice said that it might be the same group that attacked the World Trade Center with a car bomb years before. That time the plot had been botched, and a major disaster had been avoided. This time there would be no such luck. There would be many deaths.

I nearly jumped out of my chair. What did he mean, 'many deaths'? Late-night people like janitors, the cleaning crew, right?

His next words slammed into my head like a two-ton

wrecking ball.

"The first plane struck the North Tower at 8:46 a.m.," the voice said. "The business day was in full swing–offices were filled with thousands of workers. The second one at 9:01, just moments ago, would be even more catastrophic. There could be no escape for anyone on or above the point of impact. The only chance for those in offices below would be a miracle evacuation down narrow stairways–an escape route never intended for an incident of this magnitude. Hundreds–no, thousands of people would be trapped and trampled in their rush to safety."

My heart jumped into my throat. Still, I held on to the notion that Mom and Dad had never gotten to work that morning, that they were somewhere safe and would be calling the school to let me know they were okay.

The bell rang again, but the school hallways stayed empty. A second fifty-minute period began. Nobody moved. I was glued to the monitor and the voices of the reporters. I watched as the camera showed fires raging in both buildings and one enormous black cloud rolling into the Atlantic.

The screen showed people standing on Manhattan streets. Everyone was gaping at the unbelievable sight. Then, at 9:59 a.m., Dad's tower collapsed. The top floors dropped, slowly first, then with tremendous force the whole building crumpled like one of those implosions you see on the History Channel—when old places are blown up so that something new can be built in its place.

Cameras in the street showed dust clouds rushing past hundreds of people who, moments before, had been staring as dazed onlookers. Now, instead of spectators, they were running for their lives.

The reporters said that it would be only a matter of time before the other tower collapsed. Sure enough, half an hour later at 10:28 a.m., Mom's building dropped the same way Dad's had.

I knew right then, it was one way or the other: either Mom and Dad were both okay, driving home, watching a television, or they were burned, crushed and killed, either instantly by the planes' impacts or in the collapse of steel and concrete that followed.

Suddenly, I couldn't breathe. My classroom was spinning and I was falling out of my chair. Gabe Wrobel caught me and eased me into my seat. He propped me up and held on until blood returned to my head. I looked back at the screen.

The TV guys were talking about two other planes hijacked at the same time. A jumbo jet had plowed into the Pentagon and the other had crashed in a Pennsylvania farm field. The cameras switched from one scene to the next.

When the monitor focused again on Manhattan, it looked like the aftermath of World War III. A camera mounted on a helicopter showed smoke and fire everywhere. Other buildings, standing close to the Twin Towers, but not struck directly by the planes, were also demolished, their windows blown in by the immense explosive forces.

Finally, I looked around the room. Some of the kids were sitting at their desks, heads in their hands, bodies shaking. Others were standing in twos or threes–squeezing each other like that was the only way they could keep themselves from falling down. Gabe was still holding me as he watched the screen. He knew my parents worked at the Twin Towers and recognized what I was too scared to think about. I kept telling myself it would be okay, so he kept quiet and held on.

Just then the TV went black.

Chapter Four

Prom the hallway outside my room I heard shouts. I looked through the glass door and saw a boy dart past. Two girls followed him, each screaming as they ran by. When it was quiet again I looked back at the blank screen. There was a popping sound, and once again, I saw Principal Brock's face.

"All students. Please remain seated," he said grimly. "Do not leave your desks. As you have witnessed, a catastrophe has occurred. Soon you will be advised where and how to proceed. I will now turn off the TV feed, but will ask each of the teachers to leave the monitor on stand-by and await further instructions."

My head was numb. I wanted to believe this was some sort of test. But the voices–the TV guys and Mr. Brock–they were all real. All of it had to be happening.

I kept telling myself that Mom and Dad were okay–that they hadn't even gotten to work before it happened. But that didn't wash because I knew they both were sticklers for being at their desks early. They told me I should never be late for anything, whether it was school or work or even ball practice. If I wasn't interested enough to be on time, then I shouldn't be doing whatever it was I was there to do. Being prompt showed respect for your teachers, bosses, teammates—everyone.

There was no doubt: Mom and Dad would have been at their desks way before the first plane struck. One of them, and probably both, had been trapped in that smoking pile of wreckage.

Moments later the TV came back on. Mr. Brock said, "I am asking that any student who has a family member working anywhere in Manhattan to move to your classroom door. Wait

23

there until a staff person escorts you to the media center. The rest of you, please remain seated."

I walked in a daze to the door. So did a girl and another boy.

A few minutes later, the basketball coach, Mr. Fowler, stepped into our classroom. He looked at Mr. Adams, who nodded to the three of us. Coach Fowler turned, motioned for us to follow, and we left the room.

In the hall, groups of kids were walking with an adult—a librarian, secretary or custodian. All moved like zombies to the media room.

After several minutes, Mr. Brock came and stood beneath the TV screen. He cleared his throat and said slowly, "I'm afraid I have very bad news. To put aside any doubt, what you have been watching is real. The evacuation of the World Trade Center is going on as we speak. Thousands of people have been rescued, but many have not. You have been asked to come here because there is a chance you have a family member involved.

"The superintendent has cancelled all Eastham schools for the rest of the day. Buses will be arriving to take the other students home, but for your own protection, we cannot allow any of you to leave this room until we are certain that your family members are safe. We are calling your parents and asking that someone come to escort you home. Until an approved person—a parent or guardian—arrives, I must insist that you stay here for as long as it takes to ensure your safe passage."

He left the room, and as he did, the TV came back on. The reporters spoke quietly. I listened for anything that might sound like good news. From where I sat I could see the school parking lot. Buses were coming, loading and leaving.

By two o'clock, the last bus drove away. I sat in my chair and watched the TV. Hour after hour, it showed replays of the jumbo jet plowing into the South Tower while the other building smoked nearby.

One reporter summed it up. "America has been attacked. This was not an accident but a deliberate act of aggression committed by the Middle Eastern terrorist group known as al-Qaeda. Its leader is a Muslim by the name of Osama bin Laden. The group's apparent motive is retaliation against the United States for its occupation of the Arabian Peninsula and America's supposed aggression toward the Iraqi people. Today's assault is also undoubtedly in response to America's continued support of Israel, an avowed foe of Muslim ideals."

As I watched the TV, I kept one eye on the door, hoping it would swing open. Mom and Dad would be here any minute. Instead, other parents came, hugged their kid and left. My eyes would go back to the screen until the next parent rushed in. I soon began paying more attention to the door than the TV. I felt my stomach churn every time it opened.

Time dragged. Still no Mom or Dad.

Finally, during some repeat footage of the Pennsylvania farm field, I looked around the room. It was empty, except for Mr. Brock and me. He was standing by the door, watching me and talking quietly into his cell phone. When he saw me looking his way, he clicked it off and walked slowly toward me. He opened his mouth to speak, but I held up my hand.

"No, don't say it," I said, my voice trembling. I wanted to get up and run but I couldn't move. "Please, don't tell me. I already know."

He brought a chair close to me and sat down. "I'm sorry, Michael," he said. "When we didn't hear from your parents my secretary tried to call your home. All phone lines have been jammed for two hours. A few minutes ago she drove to your house. Your uncle is there. He was beside himself, not knowing how to reach you. He told her that your father called him after the first plane struck your mother's building. He said your father felt the plane's impact, ran to his window and saw flames where he knew your mother would have been sitting. Michael, your mother would have died instantly. Your father then called your uncle and told him that he had been ordered to evacuate, but that he might be late. He said to take care of you until he got home. Just as he said this, your uncle looked at his TV and saw the second jet fly into the south tower. At that moment, his phone transmission to your father went dead."

I looked up at Mr. Brock. He took a handkerchief from his jacket pocket and wiped my face.

"Michael," he said softly, "our records show that your father's office was ten floors above where the plane struck. I'm afraid that neither of your parents has survived. I will take you home. Your uncle is there waiting for you."

I started to stand but everything was spinning so fast I fell back to my chair. Mr. Brock reached down to help me. As I tried again to get to my feet, hatred of the terrorists and fear of what might happen next fought for space in my head. Who were these foreign freaks? What had Mom and Dad done to them? Well, if they were looking for an enemy, they'd found one. The US will go over there and blow their stupid little third-world country off the map.

But what am I going to do? Uncle Sean is all the family I have left. He'll go back to London, and what'll I do? I can't stay here by myself.

We walked down the long, empty hallway toward the school parking lot. I got to thinking that maybe Uncle had made a mistake. Maybe I'll get home and Mom and Dad will be there, sitting in the kitchen. Everything will be okay.

Mr. Brock helped me into his car. I slumped into the passenger seat, closed my eyes and began to rock—back and forth, back and forth. I wanted to roll myself into a ball and fall into the deepest, blackest hole in the universe.

Finally, I opened my eyes. He was driving along the same

streets I walked every day, but everything looked different. The houses, the trees, the people all looked weird.

We were getting close to my house when I thought: No, it won't be okay. I'll get there but my parents would not. They never would. Never again.

Mr. Brock turned onto my street. I looked out the window as we passed Joey Cardle's house. Last year's fight flashed through my head. I saw Joey jumping in front of me, Andy running away, me, ducking Joey's punch, and then me, landing my own. I saw Joey going down, unconscious. It seemed like a thousand years ago.

Mr. Brock's car pulled into our driveway. Uncle Sean was standing on our front porch. I got out and ran to him.

Uncle Sean held me close, saying nothing, his chest heaving. I felt wetness dropping onto my neck. We went inside and I ran straight up to my room. I slammed the door and closed the blinds. I threw myself into my bed and buried myself under the covers. I shut out all light and sound until it was like I was in my own tomb.

I rewound the tape of the whole day and saw in my mind the plane slamming into Mom's office. I watched as she was crushed and burned to death by the flaming fuselage. I saw my dad staring from his desk as it happened and him standing there, watching the whole thing.

Then I realized: He could have gotten out. He could have run for the elevator and been on the ground before the second plane struck. But he didn't. He could be here right now. He could have picked me up at school, and I wouldn't have had to sit there forever, alone. Of course, Mom didn't have a chance. She was killed in a flash, but Dad could have gotten out. He would be okay right now if he'd only been thinking. Why didn't he make a run for it while he could?

I pounded my fists into the bed. I banged my head on the bedpost. I cried myself to sleep for the first time since I was a baby.

Even before the sun had set, I had the worst nightmare of my life. It wasn't the "Giant Joey" one like before. Instead it was the three of us—Mom, Dad and me. We were standing on the World Trade Center roof. I saw a tiny speck way off in the distance. It started getting bigger. Pretty soon I could tell it was a jet, and it was coming straight for us. I started running back and forth across the roof, trying to find a way down. Mom stood there watching, like it was no use to do anything. Dad stayed with her, holding her hand. As the nose of the plane was about to slam into us, I looked into the cockpit and saw Joey Cardle at the controls. He wore a black turban and was laughing like a demented madman.

I woke up, standing in the middle of my bedroom. I was screaming my head off. Uncle Sean had me in his arms. For a second I thought it was Dad, and I felt better, like the whole day had been one terrible dream. Then Uncle said something and I knew it wasn't Dad. In an instant, everything came back. I hated Dad for quitting on me. I started throwing punches at Uncle Sean. He held me close until I wore myself out. Then I looked up at him. Tears were streaming down his cheeks.

Without another word, he walked me to my bed. He laid me down, took off my shoes, and tucked me in like I was a little baby.

I went back to sleep. I woke up when, hours later, I heard someone knocking on my door. Uncle Sean told me he'd made supper. I didn't answer him. I didn't want to eat—or live. I only wanted Mom and Dad home, safe and alive.

The next morning I awakened to the sound of Uncle Sean shouting at someone. I came down the stairs. All the shades were drawn and the house was dark. I went to Dad's den. The TV was on, flashing scenes of Manhattan, everything destroyed and smoldering. Uncle Sean slammed the phone down. He looked old and tired. His eyes were bleary. I figured he'd probably been drinking all night.

"This cussed thing has been ringing off the hook," he said, holding the phone. "Everyone wants something from you, or to give you something, or to have you go somewhere."

And he was right. I sat the whole day in front of the TV while he answered one call after another: people from my school, the county, and two churches. One was Catholic, my Dad's, and the other Protestant, my Mom's. One guy said I had to see a shrink right away. There was even someone from a funeral home, saying he would do my parents' services for free.

And there were lawyers. My parents didn't have wills. They needed me to sort through all that stuff, like I would know anything about it.

Then there were real estate guys. The house, which I guess was mine now, would eventually have to be sold. They wanted to leave their name for when I was ready to sell.

That night I had that same dream, Mom, Dad and me on the WTC roof. Just like the first time, I woke up screaming. Uncle Sean was holding me and then tucking me back into bed.

On Friday the 14th, Uncle got a call from Mr. Brock. Madison High was going to re-open. Mr. Brock would pick me up himself and bring me. I told Uncle there was no way. I couldn't even think about it. I watched TV all day, but all it showed was stuff I'd already seen and stories about the lunatics who'd done it.

Then, over the next week, our mailbox got flooded with envelopes. Money came from all over the place–grade school PTAs, churches, Rotary Clubs. For a while I thought it was nice that so many folks wanted to help kids like me. But Uncle Sean said he'd already filled an entire education account with cash, trusts, CDs, you name it. He said that taking care of it would be a full time job. As bad as things were, he told me, now I could go to any school I wanted.

What I wanted was to have Mom and Dad back, but that wasn't going to happen. All the wishing and all the money in the world couldn't do that.

I was glad Uncle Sean was there to sort through it all. I only wished Dad was here, like he could have been. Still, I don't know what I'd have done without Uncle. Pretty soon, I figured, I'd have to face that, too.

Chapter Five

~~~

The next day, Saturday the 15th, Uncle Sean said that a man had called from Washington, DC. The guy said President Bush wanted me to be with him for a speech near Ground Zero. I told Uncle Sean that I didn't think I could do that, be so close to where Mom and Dad were killed. Uncle said I had to. He said I owed it to my father, that Dad would be proud of me. I should show the world that Americans, even kids like me, would not be bullied by foreign terrorists.

Finally, I said I would, but I really didn't want to. On the morning of Sunday the 16th, in front of a solid mass of TV cameras, I got up on a stage with Mr. Bush and Mayor Giuliani. All around us were dozens of police and firemen. As I looked into the pile of wreckage, I knew that somewhere in the middle of it were my mother and father—crushed, mangled, burned and dead. There were breaks, probably for ads, when the cameras would stop and someone would come along and take a towel to my face. I don't remember much, but I've seen film, and there I was, blubbering like a baby. All around me people were giving speeches and singing songs. I hated it.

A few days later, another government official came to our house and told Uncle Sean that something would have to be done about me. He said that, since Uncle held only a visitors permit, he couldn't stay in the country much longer. I'd have to be put in a foster home. The only way around that was for Uncle Sean to become my legal guardian. He could take me to live in England. The man said he'd give us some time to think about it, but with all the terrorist talk, the state department was closing a lot of doors to visitors.

31

I said, "Why can't I just live here at my house?" The guy said it wasn't legal, that I was too young. Uncle said they should bend a rule and let him stay at his brother's house–just to take care of me until things got worked out. The guy said the government had become very strict about foreigners since 9/11. It was one or the other for me: foster home in New York or move to England with Uncle.

I didn't want to leave my school and friends. They were all I had left. I looked at Uncle. He stared at me like he didn't like the idea either, but that's not what he told the guy. He said, "I'll sign the papers and take Michael to London. My flat's not much of a place for a kid, but if that's our only choice, I'll do it."

I knew he and Mom never saw eye to eye, and he knew that I knew it, too. He was just doing it for Dad.

So that's what happened. Uncle became my guardian and the government guy said we'd have to leave no later than thirty days from then. Now, I had to go. I couldn't change my mind and live in foster care even if I wanted.

And there were the dreams. Almost every night, I'd wake up standing in the middle of my room, screaming with all my might and Uncle would be holding me in his arms. Every night it was the same. He'd put me back in bed and tuck me in.

And every day, every place I went, there'd be TV cameras with plastic-faced, microphone-stabbing reporters shoving their way in front of me, wanting me to say something. That was the worst, them asking me how I felt about losing my parents. What a stupid question. Then they'd ask what I thought about al-Qaeda, like now I was some sort of expert on foreign maniacs. They wanted my opinion on President Bush sending troops to Afghanistan, and what France was or wasn't doing about the terrorists.

The first few times caught me off guard. I wondered why they'd care what I thought. I mean, me, a thirteen-year-old kid. I tried to answer them, but all they really wanted to know was how I felt, having both of my parents killed like that. And they always got this little tearful choke in their voices when they asked it. Then I figured it out: I was news. I was a moving target and they wanted credit for catching me in their sights. What a bunch of phonies.

So, for about a week, my picture was plastered over every magazine, newspaper and website. Finally, like Joey Cardle's Demons, I discovered that TV people had pretty short attention spans too. They soon lost interest in me and found other folks to pester.

When it got to be too much, I'd take it out on Uncle Sean. I forgot he had lost as much as I had: his only living family member, besides me of course. Still, he was there for everything—the funerals, the trips to Ground Zero, the speeches—everything.

I turned fourteen on Tuesday, September 18th, exactly one week after my parents were killed. It was the first birthday I'd ever had that Mom didn't bake a cake and the three of us would go to a Mets or a Yankees game, whichever team was in town. It was that day that it sunk in: I was going to have to live the rest of my life without them. How I coped would be all up to me. I realized that I wasn't the first kid in the world to have something like this happen–having his parents die suddenly and to be an orphan. I remembered Dad saying, "If something doesn't kill you, it makes you stronger." Well, I was still alive, so I guess I'd be stronger because of it.

On Wednesday the 19th, Uncle Sean asked me if I was ready to go.

"Right now?" I said. "I mean, we still got three weeks."

"Aye, but there's things I must attend back home," Uncle said.

I wanted to put it off, but I knew the day would come sooner or later. "All right," I said. "Might as well be now."

He made a bunch of phone calls. A truck came and four men hauled all my parents' stuff out of the house–took it to some liquidation place. They gave Uncle a check and he put it in a folder.

The next day a real estate man and a bank guy came. They talked for a while and walked through the house. The place had gotten a little messy with just Uncle and me living there, but finally the bank guy gave Uncle Sean a check. He stuck that in the folder, too.

Two days later, on Friday the 21st, we packed our bags. Uncle tossed Dad's little trail guitar into its case and put it with our luggage.

I looked at the guitar. "What are we taking that for?" I asked.

He said, "It'll give you something to do with your time. Besides, music is good for the soul."

"I don't feel much like singing," I told him, but we brought it anyway.

We got in the taxi and went to the airport. What a zoo that was. Soldiers with bulletproof jackets, helmets and assault rifles walked shoulder to shoulder outside each gate. Guards with metal detectors were everywhere. Customs guys who only glanced at my passport last year when we flew to Bermuda now took a magnifying glass to every paper I had. Lines of people snaked through the terminal.

Uncle Sean, with his British papers and Irish birth certificate, got so mad at this one guy that he nearly took a swing at him. But then another uniform saw that I was with him. He recognized us from all the TV interviews. He checked our tickets and papers and walked us straight through to the plane.

Finally, four hours late, we took off. I sat back in the seat and it sank in. I was leaving everything I had ever known: school, friends, home, sports, everything—maybe forever. Usually I get a little nervous when the plane is barreling down the runway and about to take off. It seems like that's when most accidents happen, the plane can't climb above a tree or a house, something like that, and then it crashes. But this time I just leaned back and closed my eyes. It was like I didn't care. Life couldn't get much worse. I slept most of the way, getting up only to go to the bathroom and scarf down a sandwich. Luckily, I didn't have one of my nightmares.

Uncle nudged me when we landed in London. I was still half asleep when we went through Customs. We picked up our bags and forced our way through the crowd to a passenger train. The fifteen-minute ride got us to Victoria Station. I looked out the window. The place was jammed with more British Army soldiers and security guards than travelers. It seemed like the whole world was on Red Alert.

I grabbed my duffel bag and guitar and ran to keep up with Uncle Sean as he hurried to an exit. We went down some long stairs and crammed ourselves into a subway car.

After a bumpy, twisting ride, we came to Kilburn Station. Just as I had pushed myself into the train, I had to push my way out.

On the platform, people shoved me along while I clung to my luggage. It was like being caught in a swollen river, moving faster and faster until suddenly, we were on an escalator. A minute later I was nearly shot out of the station and into the street.

The raw sunlight scorched my eyes. Uncle hailed a cab and we climbed in. I stared out the window as the taxi moved slowly through the traffic. We didn't go far, but as we drove along the trash-strewn streets I noticed that there were no lawns or gardens. A few spindly trees grew wild here and there, but they were too sparse and far apart to give any shade. All I saw was one drab apartment complex after another with only an occasional, brightly colored front door to break the monotony.

Then the cab came to a stop. I got out and found myself standing in a filthy alley barely a car's width across. Uncle pointed to a decrepit, three-story row house and said, "This is it."

I stared at the place. If this was it, it was pretty grim.

I looked up and down the street. Burglarproof, iron bars were bolted to every door and window on Willesden Lane. Most were rusted and covered with windblown plastic shopping bags. Graffiti was everywhere. The whole place looked like parts of New York City where I would never have set foot, much less stayed. It was like a war zone.

I wondered why I had pictured London as being so wonderful. Maybe I'd watched too many Disney movies, but I quickly got the feeling I had made a huge mistake. I should never have left New York. I wished I hadn't decided so fast. I mean, no foster home in America could be this bad. It wasn't like I would have much control back home, but here I would have none. I was a foreigner now. In New York I knew where I could go and where I couldn't. Here, I didn't have a clue.

Cars flew by on the wrong side of the street. Traffic signs were nothing more than unrecognizable symbols. How could anyone know what they meant? People spoke English, but with such weird accents I couldn't understand a word they said.

"Welcome to Little Belfast," Uncle Sean said. "The Kilburn Road, this part of London, is your new home."

I'm sure he didn't mean it this way, but it sounded like a death sentence. A sinking feeling washed over me. I was a rowboat adrift on the ocean. The next wave would send me to the bottom.

I looked again at the pathetic building. This is home? This isn't anything like home.

I hated this place.

I hated the terrorists who'd hijacked the planes and slammed them into the Twin Towers.

I hated Dad for not getting out when he could.

I hated Uncle for bringing me here.

I hated everything.

Chapter Six

Uncle Sean unlocked the door and I went inside. As I set my bags on the floor, Uncle fell into his well-worn, stuffed easy chair, the one directly in front of an old eighteen-inch TV. He nodded for me to sit in the other. I did.

"Gotta see what the mood is," he said. He clicked on the TV. I watched, but it wasn't any different than at home. Every channel showed nothing but 9/11 stuff: warnings about terrorists and what to watch for, suitcases left on the ground or people asking you to hold a package for them as you passed through Customs.

My eyes drifted around the apartment. It was small and shabby, no bigger that our two-car garage back home. I got to wondering why Uncle Sean had ended up in London and my parents had gone to America. So I asked him.

"Michael," he said, "I don't know how much you know about your parents, how they got together, but I have a feeling they never told you their story."

"Their story? What do you mean?"

"Did you ever wonder why two people would pick up, leave their home country and go to the United States?" he asked.

"Lots of people do," I said. "Been going on for years." I shrugged. "I don't know, maybe their companies transferred them?"

He shook his head. "Not even close. When they left Ireland, they quit their jobs in Belfast and got on a boat. They carried practically nothing but the clothes on their backs, a few things stuffed into a couple duffle bags."

"Maybe they had friends in New York, people who had a job waiting for them."

"No," Uncle said. "When they got to America they started from scratch. They knew nobody. Your dad scrubbed floors in a building owned by an advertising company. The brass liked how hard he worked, not to mention his gift of gab, or blarney, which is what the Irish are known for in America. The company had this deal where they gave money to their workers for schooling. Not many janitors took them up on it, but Brendan did. In a few years he worked his way into sales. Not long after that he was their top salesman."

"I guess Dad was a pretty smart guy," I said.

"You have no idea," Uncle said. "This was years before you were born, of course. And did you ever wonder about your dad being Catholic and your mum being Protestant, how they got together?"

"I never thought to ask," I said. "We never talked about religion at home. Some of my friends were Jewish, but I only know that because, at Christmas, we had a tree and they had a Menorah. Other kids were from India, China—all over the place. At school we didn't talk about religion, at least not in class. I knew Mom was Presbyterian and Dad was Roman Catholic, but why would that matter?"

"Michael," Uncle said, "for each of your parents, religion, or at least the politics behind it, would have meant everything to them. In cities like Belfast, your religion was who you were. It was the first thing you found out about anyone you met. Everything depended on it. That was because of the Troubles."

"Wait," I said. "You and Dad used to talk about that. It doesn't sound very serious. I mean, trouble is what I get into if I skip school or break a window, stuff like that."

Uncle shook his head. "It's something entirely different in

Ireland," he said. "In Ireland, the Troubles is synonymous with War—the English government against the Irish people. Years ago, your dad was one of the Irish Republican Army's young bloods. He did things that made him a legend. Oh, aye, Brendan was active during the Troubles, sure he was."

"Active?" I said. "I'm active in school, you know, sports and clubs. You make it sound like being active is a crime."

"In Belfast being active had nothing to do with school," Uncle said. "And it could get you killed, like it did a lot of my friends and, except for Brendan and me, the whole rest of our family. Your dad must never have told you this, but our family was murdered—our mum and pa, two sisters and little brother, all for something Brendan did."

"Something my father did?" I said. I stared at Uncle Sean. "Dad never said anything about that. You're joking, right?"

"No," Uncle Sean said, staring back.

We looked at each other for almost a minute while I tried to sort all this out. I wasn't sure I wanted to hear any more, but I asked anyway. "All right," I said, "since Dad never told me about it, I guess I'd better hear it from you. Let's start with this: What exactly were the Troubles?"

Uncle Sean looked at me like he didn't know where to start. "It goes back a bit," he said, "all the way to the 1100s. But in 1534, it got worse. That's when Henry VIII decided to divorce his first wife, Catherine of Aragon. She happened to be the aunt of the Emperor of Spain, King Charles V. At that time, Spain *was* Europe. The Spanish Empire was more powerful than puny little England. It had a bigger army, stronger navy, more land. It was *the* world power.

"Henry decided that, in order for England to remain sovereign, he needed to have a son to take over for him when he died. Henry and Catherine had one child, a daughter. Princess Mary would eventually take over the throne when Henry died. Henry didn't think she, as queen, could lead an army into battle like a king could. He wanted a son.

"Catherine got old without having any more children, so Henry decided he would divorce her. He would get a new wife who could have more babies—sons, preferably. Henry had his eye on this young bird in his court, Ann Boleyn. He wanted her to be his new wife, but divorce was strictly against Roman Catholic rules. The Pope in Rome, who had Spain's backing, would never allow it. Are you getting the picture?"

"Yeah," I said. "Henry was up against it, right?"

"Right," Uncle said. "Kings in general, and Henry in particular, weren't big on taking no for an answer. Henry decided to do things his way. He started his own church, which would still be Catholic, but it wouldn't be Roman Catholic. He called it the Church of England. He would be its pope and make new rules. The first rule he changed was to make divorce legal. The second thing he did was divorce Catherine of Aragon. So, her nephew, Spain's King Charles, made plans to send his Spanish Armada over to England to bounce Henry off the throne and take over the whole country."

"All right," I said, "but what does this have to do with Ireland?"

"We're getting there," Uncle said. "Real Irish people, Roman Catholics like us, threw our support to the Spanish Emperor, Charles. King Henry saw the danger of Ireland teaming up with Spain who could use Ireland as a jumping off place for an attack on England. Henry sent his soldiers to crush us and teach us not to mess with him, but pretty soon he found out that the Irish were fighting back. Henry decided he'd show us who was boss. He gathered his most ruthless English friends and sent them to Ireland to be our landlords. They put every Catholic Irish man, woman and child into slavery—those they didn't kill first. Henry gave his pals the power to do anything they wanted to us. These 'lords' built forts and brought soldiers to make sure Henry's orders were carried out."

"Just like that?" I said. "Like overnight?"

"Aye," Uncle answered. "We became slaves to the king and made to work our old fields, which now belonged to these lords. These were fields we'd owned and handed down from father to son for generations. Next, the king's Parliament passed the Penal Laws, which made it illegal for us to speak Gaelic, our native language. We couldn't go to our own Roman Catholic Church. We had to pray in King Henry's Anglican ones. We couldn't own land or horses. We were treated worse than animals. Horses were fed better, pigs, too. We were made to do the worst things that the king's tyrants could dream up. And if any Irishman didn't like the rules, he'd be hanged."

"Why did you take it?" I asked. "Didn't anyone fight back?"

"Sure, we fought back," Uncle said. "Catholic priests, who the Protestant landlords considered more evil than the Devil himself, held mass in fields, huts, anywhere they could. Teachers walked from town to town and taught children to read and write, but never in the open. They had to hide behind hedgerows. If they were caught, they'd be killed on the spot. Dads and mums passed the Gaelic tongue to their babies with stories and songs, each showing our hatred for England and their murdering landlords."

"Come on," I said. "It couldn't have been that bad."

"Oh, aye, that it was," Uncle said. "The lords sent their henchmen out and arrested anyone they wanted, little boys and girls as likely as men and women. They'd be tortured and made to tell names of people who had put them up to their so-called crimes. Then those people would be tracked down, caught, tortured and murdered."

"I can't believe this," I said. I was thinking maybe I was hearing one side of a two-sided story, sort of like at my trial with Joey Cardle and how the fast-talking lawyers made it sound like I was the bad guy. But Uncle Sean sounded so sure of himself. "Wasn't there anything the people could do?" I asked.

"Not much," Uncle said. "Oh, it wasn't like we didn't try, but the king had swords and cannons. We had sticks and stones. The king had horses and forts. We had pigs and huts. In all the years since Henry VIII, with just a couple exceptions, it's been the same. The English have beaten us down at every turn. So, for centuries, every chance we could give aid to England's enemy, whoever it was at the time, we did. And that's included Spain, the American colonies, France—even Germany."

"Wait! You can't be serious," I said. "The Irish helped Hitler?"

"Aye, the real Irish–us Roman Catholics," Uncle said. "And we sided with Kaiser Wilhelm before Hitler. In 1916 during World War I, Germany had taken over most of Europe and was all set to invade England. Kaiser Wilhelm told Ireland that he would spare us if we didn't help England. When the British government heard about this, Parliament decided to promise the Irish that if our men joined the British army, Ireland could have its independence when the war was over. That's how desperate England was. We figured it was an empty promise, but thousands of Irishmen enlisted on the chance Germany might go back on its word, which they'd done to other countries like Austria and Poland. So we put on the hated British uniform, went off to war, and died by the thousands, carrying the Union Jack to the front lines. We were nothing more than cannon fodder for German snipers and artillery men.

"When the United States got into the war the tide turned quickly. Germany lost, but even so, England only half lived up to its promise to allow Ireland its freedom. In 1922 three quarters of Ireland became the Irish Free State, still a part of the British Empire, but with some freedoms they didn't have before. Six counties in the north of Ireland, the province of Ulster, which is mostly Scots-Irish, king-loving Protestants, they voted to stick with England. Those six counties became Northern Ireland. Life there was fine for the Protestants, but for any Catholics in cities like Derry and Belfast, it was a living hell."

"You mean it got worse?" I asked.

"Aye, that it did," Uncle said. "There, in the North, the Protestants, or Prods, that's what we called your mother's people, controlled everything. And every year it got worse. The Prods said to us Catholics, 'All right, you've got your Irish Free State, go live there.' What few good jobs the Northern Ireland Catholics had, they lost. We got burned out of our homes and treated like swine. We took it, but we didn't take it lying down."

I stared at Uncle. It sure sounded like the English had kicked the Irish around for a long time. Was this just Uncle's version of the two-sided story? I'd find out soon.

Chapter Seven

~~~~~~

Istared at Uncle Sean as he got more and more worked up. I wondered why Dad or Mom hadn't told me this. Maybe my father was ashamed of himself for running off to America and not staying to help the Cause. Maybe Mom was ashamed of Dad for being such a trouble-causing rebel. Anyway, all of this was news to me.

"So, why didn't your dad get out?" I asked. "Why didn't he go to the Irish Free State?"

"Look at it this way," Uncle Sean said. "Let's say you're a man and you have a family. You've got a job. It's horrible work and way beneath your abilities, but it's the only way you can put food on the table and clothe your family. So, what would you do, stay in the North and eke out a living, or move to a place in the South of Ireland—Dublin, Limerick, Cork—where you may not find any work at all?"

"Couldn't your dad just put everyone on a boat and go to America?"

Uncle scoffed. "Seven people on his wages? Don't be daft."

"All right," I said, "I guess I'd stay in Belfast and work, but I wouldn't be happy about it."

"Well, that's what Pa did," Uncle Sean said. "And he wasn't happy. But he stuck to his family. My brother was different. Without Pa knowing it, Brendan joined the IRA and made up for all of us. He fought the bloody English like the Devil himself."

"Wow," I said. I was stunned. "So, your family lived like

that, always under England's thumb?"

"Every moment," Uncle Sean said. "The Prods got the best of everything: high-paying work, nice homes. We got the scraps: backbreaking jobs, slum housing. The Prods let us have just enough to live on and never a morsel to spare."

"So, the Troubles, that's when the lid blew off, right?"

"Aye. It festered for years until the mid-'60s," Uncle said. "It was at the same time the United States was going through its own Troubles. Americans called it the Civil Rights Movement. Black people like Martin Luther King, Malcolm X, Rosa Parks were fighting for their own equality. They did it by protesting. They marched, gave speeches, staged sit-ins. White folksingers, Pete Seeger, Woody Guthrie, and black ones like Josh White and Huddie Ledbetter wrote songs telling how unfair conditions were. They'd get arrested and thrown in jail, get themselves on TV.

"In Ireland, we saw what they were doing and that it was working. We started to do the same thing, hunger strikes, marches, protest songs, everything we could to show how bad the English were treating us."

"You're right, Uncle," I said. "It is hard to believe. Are you saying that the riots that went on in Ireland during the 1970s started because of America's Civil Rights Movement in the '60s?"

"That's just what I'm saying," Uncle said. "I told you about being 'active' in the IRA. If you lived in Belfast, it meant that by the time you were ten, you'd be marching and waving anti-British signs along the Falls Road. That's where a lot of us Catholics lived. But it didn't do any good. British soldiers shot at us with rubber bullets. For revenge an IRA man might toss a gasoline bomb into a Prod business. It went on day after day. One night, someone saw Brendan near a blast, so, like about a hundred other blokes, he was brought in by the RUC."

"You're kidding. Wait a minute. What's the RUC?" I asked.

"The Royal Ulster Constabulary," Uncle said, "the Northern Irish police force. They were supposed to be made up of an equal number of Catholics and Protestants, but any Catholic who joined the force, the IRA figured he was a traitor. So, none of us did. The RUC became just another name for a bunch of Prod thugs in cop clothes. If the RUC thought someone might be part of one of those bombings, they'd bring him in and beat him bloody."

"Well, that never happened to Dad, right?"

"Oh, aye. That it did," Uncle said. "One night, your dad, he was fifteen, he and his mate pipe-bombed a Prod fish shop on the Shankhill Road. The RUC came to our house and dragged him off—for questioning, they said. We didn't think we'd ever see him again—not alive, anyway."

"But you did," I said.

"Of course," Uncle said. "Brendan got away, but only because they couldn't prove it. Also, he wouldn't give the names of the IRA men behind it."

"So, the pipe bomb, was anyone hurt?" I asked.

"At the fish shop? Aye, of course," Uncle said. "A dozen Prods were killed."

I stared in disbelief. "You can't be serious," I said. "My father killed twelve people?"

"Oh, aye," Uncle said with a nod. "The RUC tortured Brendan for over a week. He came home a bloody mess, he did, but he never confessed. They let him go, but from then on they hounded every step he took."

I shook my head, not fathoming any of this. "You keep talking about the IRA," I said. "What is the IRA?"

Uncle looked bewildered at my ignorance. "The Irish Republican Army," he said. "Goes back a hundred years. It's mostly men but there are women too. We want Ireland to run by the Irish and I mean all of Ireland, North and South, like it was a thousand years ago. Some want to use politics to do it, get voted into office and pass new laws, but that's failed so many times that we know the only real way is to use force. That's where we come in, the IRA militants, the Provisional wing—the Provos."

"So, Dad was a Provo?" I asked.

"Aye, that he was, one of the boldest, fiercest, most trusted IRA men in all of Ireland," Uncle said. "He did the dirty work to make our people free."

I sat back in my chair. Finally, I shook my head. "Come on, Uncle," I said. "Dad would never have done any of that stuff— throw rocks at police, set off bombs, kill people. I mean, he'd tan my butt if I'd so much as frown at a crossing guard."

"Brendan did everything I told you and much, much more," Uncle Sean said. "Besides that, he lit the fire under our troops by singing Rebel protest songs. That little six-string you have," he said, nodding to my guitar case, "stirred up more mayhem than a dozen pipe bombs put together. He sang at IRA meetings all over the North."

I looked at the beat-up guitar case next to my duffel bag. "That was Dad's?" I asked. "I never saw him play it, not even once. I just thought he kept it for you."

"Oh, he played it, all right," Uncle said. "He was brilliant. Every night, he'd grab my arm and we'd go to secret IRA meetings. At first, it was just around Belfast. Then the IRA captains took us to towns like Lurgan, Ardglass, Newry. There was this one time, in Newry it was. Brendan finished one of his songs, and while the boys were shouting their hurrahs and stamping their feet, one of them jumped up, ran outside and shot the first Tommy, that's an English soldier, shot the first Tommy he saw."

"You're kidding."

"Michael, it's a bloody fact."

"Well, that wasn't Dad's fault," I said. "I mean, Dad didn't shoot the guy."

"Didn't matter to the RUC. They came after him," Uncle said. "Early that next morning, about four o'clock, some IRA men gave Brendan and me a ride back to Belfast. They dropped us off a few blocks from our tenement house like they always did. It was safer for the drivers and us both. We were thirty yards from home when we saw a car driving slowly along our street. It pulled up at our front door. Three men got out, all carrying machine guns. Brendan grabbed my arm and pulled me between two buildings. We watched as the blokes smashed the door and ran in. They lit up our whole place, room by room, with hundreds of rounds of gunfire. When they came out we could tell by their faces that they'd botched the job. They'd missed their target—Brendan. Missed him and me by two minutes, they did."

Blood drained from my head. "What did you do?" I said.

"We were still crouched between the buildings when Brendan kneeled and made the sign of the cross. He grabbed me by the shirt, and we ran like rats through the alleys. Finally, we holed up until morning in a stinking garbage truck. Brendan figured that even bloodhounds couldn't track us there. We found out for sure the next day that our whole family had been slaughtered. Our mother, father, two sisters and little brother were all shot in cold blood. Brendan said it was payback for the song he'd sung the night before, for the Tommy who'd been killed. He said, 'We'll have to hide out, maybe for a long time.'"

I stared at Uncle Sean. "Dad never told me any of this," I said. "Then what did you do?"

"Brendan said the roads out of Belfast would be locked down by the RUC. Police dogs would be scouring every alley. Brendan had friends in another part of Belfast, down by the docks. They'd take us in. He told me I had to watch who I talked to or even looked at, and never draw any attention to myself, at least until the RUC gave up looking for us. Every Catholic kid our age would be brought in and grilled."

"Wait a minute," I said. "How could someone tell you were

Catholic just by looking at you? Irish Catholics and Protestants are white, aren't they?"

"Aye, of course, Michael," Uncle Sean said. "But there are other ways of telling—clothes, speech. Belfast alone has at least a dozen accents. We can tell with the first word out of a bloke's mouth what part of town he's from. And from that, we know if he's one of us or one of them."

"Uncle, sometimes I think you're pulling my leg," I said.

"Michael, it's all true. When I was growing up, it was a known fact that every Prod was a Catholic-hating, British-loving Unionist. Given the chance, they'd kill us as likely as look at us. In America, your schools lump everyone together—Muslim, Jewish, Catholic, or Protestant. Your friends could be black, white, Latino or Asian. Nobody would care. You sit in classrooms, eat lunch, play sports, do everything together, but in Belfast, we were kept completely apart. We had to know who everyone was. If I even nodded politely to some English kid, I'd be suspected of disloyalty, taken in by the IRA and questioned. And I'd better have a pretty good excuse for being friendly to a Brit, see? It was a matter of life and death."

"Didn't you even have games against each other in school sports?" I asked.

Uncle scoffed. "Our rugby or football clubs would no more play a Prod team than we would kneel in a Presbyterian pew on Sunday. Our moms went to market at Catholic-owned shops. Our dads drank their Guinness at Catholic-run pubs."

"How could you live like that?" I said.

"It's all we ever knew," Uncle Sean said. "We figured it never was or ever would be any different."

I sat back, trying to take it all in. Then I realized he still hadn't told me what I really wanted to know.

Chapter Eight

"Okay, I get all that," I said. "So, with everything you've told me about Protestants and Catholics, how much they hated each other and how they were always kept apart, how did Mom and Dad meet?"

"Right," Uncle Sean said. "After about a month of hiding at our mate's place, Brendan found work on the docks. Belfast is a shipping port, and Brendan loaded and unloaded freighters. Before the main office closed at night, he swept floors and emptied wastebaskets. Your mother was a secretary there. That's where they first saw each other. Dad knew what she was, and she knew what he was—him Catholic and her a Prod. But that didn't keep them from eyeing each other every now and then."

"Wait a minute," I said, holding up my hand. "How did she know Dad was Catholic? And how'd he know she was Protestant?"

"From their jobs," Uncle Sean said. "I told you. Your mom sat at a cushy desk in the shipping office. Brendan was doing backbreaking, manual labor. That's the way it's been for a thousand years."

"All right," I said. "I get the picture."

"Anyway, your dad was totally smitten. I could tell something was up the very first night he came home from work after seeing her. Until then he wore a scowl, like practically everyone else. It told strangers to mind their own business. He wasn't that way around me, of course, but if we were out in public, his expression told others to keep their distance.

"That night, when he walked in from work, he was grinning

50

from ear to ear. I asked him what had come over him. He told me about this awesome bird at the office. I told him, 'Brendan, she's a Prod. You know that, right? You've got to forget her.' And he said, 'I can't help it. When I look at her and she looks at me, it's like none of that other stuff matters. I can dream, can't I?' I told him, 'No, you can't dream. Dreaming is for people who don't care if they live or die.' I told him that, but Brendan wasn't listening.

"Before long, he and Anne were nodding to each other, and then openly speaking, if only to say 'Ta' or 'Cheerio.' One day, just as he was about to sweep her area, she nodded to him and dropped a piece of paper in her wastebasket. He took it to the trash bin with the others, keeping his eye on which can held her note. When no one was looking, he slipped it into his pocket.

"I was there that night when he got home. He read it and his face lit up. She wanted to meet him. She told him about a folk music club at Queen's University. Brendan and I knew about Queen's. It wasn't far from the Falls Road where we grew up. Queen's students came to Belfast from all over the world. Everyone—Brits, Chinese, Africans—they all studied together. They never worried about other students' politics or religion. Queen's was like an oasis of tolerance surrounded by a sea of prejudice. To us, it didn't seem natural, but to the students, it was just the way it was.

"Anne was taking a night class there. After it was over she would drop by the Whitla Hall for the Folk Music Society's weekly meeting. Her note said for Brendan to meet her there. She said they could talk, like they were regular students, and not raise any red flags.

"Those meetings became the most important part of Brendan's life. As an outsider he didn't belong there, so he nicked some Queen's student's blue and green school scarf. He put it on, grabbed his guitar and tried to blend in with the others. He even sang once in a while, but he was careful not to do any of his Rebel songs for fear of getting too much attention. Besides, he was just glad to be with Anne, even though the pro-English songs some of the others sang made his blood boil.

"The more he went to those meetings the happier he got. The more he wore that silly grin, the more I knew there would be trouble. I could feel it coming. After a while, Brendan lost his scowl completely. He smiled almost all the time. It made him look like he'd lost his mind. And I told him so. He told me not to worry. That was it. No one but a moron would dare be anything but afraid 'round the clock in Belfast no matter which side he was on.

"And sure enough, one day a bloke, a Prod, I could tell right away, came round our mate's flat. He asked where Brendan was. I told him I didn't know who he meant. The bloke gave me a little smirk, like he knew exactly what was going on. When the guy left, I ducked out the back door and ran to find Brendan. As soon as I saw him I said, 'You have to get out of here,' and told him why. He nodded and, just like that, his old scowl came back.

"It was Thursday. That night was the folk music meeting at Queen's. That afternoon Brendan went to the docks and hid until dark. Then he sneaked back to our mate's flat and crammed a few things into a plastic bag. He wrapped his arms around me and said, 'Don't wait up.' He grabbed his guitar and left for the meeting. He was gone.

"When he didn't come home that night, I was sure something had gone wrong. I figured the RUC had nabbed him. I knew how tough he was, but I was still afraid they'd break him. If they got it out of him where he was staying, they'd come for me. I grabbed my clothes, threw them in a bag and went down to the docks. A freighter was tied up there. I waited until the guard wasn't looking and ran up the gangplank. I hid myself in a lifeboat. I had no idea where the ship was bound, but I didn't care as long as it was away from Belfast.

"Pretty soon, I could feel the ship pitching, so I knew we were under way. I slept that night for the first time since the RUC murdered my family.

"The boat came into port the next day, and I slipped ashore.

I found myself on the streets of Liverpool.

"Luckily, I met another Irish ex-pat and holed up with him. About a month later I got word from a mate that Brendan and Anne were in America. I never did find out how they did it. Brendan told me years later that the less I knew the less I could tell. He said, 'Even old secrets can hang people.'"

Uncle Sean was done talking. He leaned back in his chair.

"So," I said, taking in a breath. "That's how Mom and Dad met. They never told me any of that."

"Your dad had a new life in America and didn't want to look back," Uncle Sean said. "When you came along, it was even easier for him to forget his old home. Every time I went to America, I tried to get him to help with the Cause, but he never did. I told him what the money was for, that the boys needed guns to break the English and make Ireland whole again. He said, 'You mean the enemy, the Protestants, like Anne's family?' He had me there, and I knew he was a lost cause, at least for my cause."

"Is it still like that in Belfast?" I asked. "All the hate and fighting?"

"Not as much," Uncle Sean said. "Since Good Friday, 1998, that's when the Belfast peace treaty was signed, both sides have cooled their heels mostly. We're all supposed to act nice to each other, but I doubt that will ever happen. British soldiers drive around Belfast streets in Hummers instead of armored tanks. They wear standard uniforms rather than combat fatigues. It's still tense, but nothing like what it was."

I asked, "And the IRA and the RUC, after all those years of beatings and bombings, they're all buddy-buddy now?"

"Michael, I don't know if Ireland, especially the North, will ever be totally at peace," he said. "For my money, it will never be over until the last Englishman leaves Ireland. And after all these years on our soil, they've gotten pretty used to pushing us around and running our lives. No, Michael, it doesn't seem likely."

As I sat in Uncle's apartment, I suddenly felt very tired. "Uncle, I think I've got a serious case of jet lag. Would it be okay if I just sacked out for a bit?"

"Sure, and I might take forty winks meself," Uncle Sean said.

He went into his bedroom and came out with a flimsy old army cot. Piled on top were a thick cotton sheet and a coarse woolen blanket. I set up the makeshift bed, spread out the blanket and settled in. It was like trying to sleep on a pile of straw, all scratchy and smelly. As I tried to get comfortable I wondered what I had gotten myself into. Would I have to watch who I talked to, be afraid of everyone? I wished I was back home and 9/11 had never happened–that Mom and Dad had never met. I even wished I'd never been born.

I curled up into a ball. I began to worry I'd wake up screaming from another nightmare. I didn't want that to happen, but you don't have much say over what you dream.

Something crashed and I woke up. I was so sound asleep that I forgot where I was. I looked around and saw pale sunlight slanting through filthy, iron-barred windows. Everything came rushing back. More loud sounds came from nearby. I rolled off the cot and found Uncle standing in the kitchen. The fridge door was wide open. He was pouring soured milk globs into the sink. Next he dropped slimy slabs of rotten fish into a huge, black plastic bag. The stench nearly brought me to my knees.

Uncle turned and saw me in the doorway. He smiled weakly. "I told you I needed to get back," he said. "Let's go out for tea. There's a wee pub nearby. It's a little bit of Belfast right here in London. You'll find more Irish Catholics here on the Kilburn Road than still live up the Falls Road back home. Grab your jacket."

"All right," I said. I used to eat out with Mom and Dad a

lot, but always at just regular restaurants. Maybe an Irish pub, even those fake ones you find in practically every strip mall in America, brought bad memories for both of them.

We left Uncle's flat and walked half a block down the street to a tiny hole-in-the-wall shop. A faded wooden sign hanging in front read, "Casey's." An eye-level window in the door was either steamed up from the inside or dirty from the outside, but either way, I couldn't see through it.

Uncle Sean didn't bother trying. He just turned the handle and barged in. I followed, stepping over a stone threshold worn down by centuries of hard-soled shoes tramping over it. I was nearly knocked backward by everything going on inside. It all happened so suddenly that it's hard to say what I noticed first.

The din inside was crushing. I stood for a second looking over Uncle's shoulder. The whole pub was hardly bigger than my kitchen back home, but it was crammed with people, forty at least. Everyone was yammering, almost screaming to be heard over everyone else. Two TVs blared in opposite corners. Heavy glasses were clanking. It was rock-concert loud.

Aside from the deafening roar, a rank odor hit me next. I would have stopped right there, but if I had, I'd have lost sight of Uncle Sean, who was elbowing his way to the bar.

Inside were six small tables, each with two or three chairs. Dozens of people were crammed between them, holding their pints of beer and glasses of whiskey. Beyond was the bar with a line of tall stools in front, all in use.

Behind the bar was Casey, as round as he was tall. He stood there, head high, filling pint glasses with beer so thick and black you'd have thought it was old, truck, crankcase oil. He wore a dingy white apron over a tweed sports jacket, a grimy white shirt open to the neck, and as pleased a look as any man you'd ever hope to see.

From here, Casey held sway over all within his realm. He personally served his bar customers, while a kid, his son, a spitting image of Casey only smaller, ran back and forth taking orders from the floor.

Uncle pulled a chair from one of the tables near the bar and motioned for me to join him. From my seat I watched for a few minutes as the boy ran sandwich orders to the back room where someone, his mom I found out, made the food.

Uncle called over to Casey and ordered a pint of Guinness for himself, a lemon mineral for me and some crisps. I didn't know what a lemon mineral was but it turned out to be a bottle of soda, sort of like sparkly lemonade. The crisps were just small bags of potato chips.

We sat there for a while until Casey spoke over the crowd to my uncle. "So, will yeh be havin' somethin' from the scullery, Sean?" he shouted.

I looked for a menu, but didn't see one. I guessed everyone knew what Casey had, everyone but me, of course.

"We'll each have a plate of sandwiches," Uncle shouted back.

"What kind, egg, cheese or hom?" Casey asked, looking first at Uncle Sean.

Uncle Sean answered, "Egg for me, Casey."

Casey then looked at me.

I really didn't want an egg or a cheese sandwich, but I didn't know what "hom" was. I figured it must be short for something, hominy grits, maybe, so I asked, "Uh, what is hom?"

Casey blinked, like he didn't understand what I was saying. He glanced over at Uncle, then back at me. Then he nodded, like he finally got it; I was a foreigner. He spoke slowly and distinctly, "Hom, you know, like what comes from a hog."

A light went on. "Oh, ham," I said. "Okay, I'll have a ham sandwich."

Uncle Sean smiled sheepishly and said, "Casey, I'd like

you to meet my nephew, Michael. He's just come with me from New York."

Casey looked at Uncle Sean, then at me, then at Uncle Sean again. Suddenly, he burst out laughing. He laughed so hard I was afraid he was going to hurt himself. Tears came to his eyes as he doubled over. You'd have thought I had just told the funniest joke ever in the history of the world.

Casey rubbed his eyes and tried to collect himself. "Oh, well, that explains everything," he said. Then he scrunched his face up into a dim-witted expression and said with a wildly fake twang, "Ay-merican, are yeh now?"

I guessed my accent must have been what he thought was so funny. "Uh, yes, sir," I said, trying not to give him another reason to go off. One more fit like the last one might do the old boy in.

"Ah, but that was good," he said, his belly still shaking. He turned to the boy and called with a nasally, country-western accent, "Liam, see if yer ma can't rustle up a couple a' them there hay-um sammiches for our Ay-merican friend."

"Two hay-um sammiches, coming up," the boy said, joining the act. Then he poked his head into the back room and shouted, "Hey, Ma, we need two hay-um sammiches out here."

By then, everyone in the place was laughing uproariously. Casey was turning red and gasping for breath.

Now, I don't usually like being the butt of a joke, but Casey was so beside himself, and he looked so funny that I started to laugh along with him.

Pretty soon everyone, I mean every person in the place started ordering hay-um sammiches, each trying to sound like some sort of ignorant hillbilly.

After I'd downed the sandwiches, potato chips and a couple more lemon minerals, I decided I needed to go to the john. "Where's the bathroom?" I asked Uncle Sean.

"You want to take a bath?" he deadpanned.

"No, I mean..."

He held up his hand and said with a smile, "I know what you mean. Here it's called the 'loo,' and it's down the way a bit," he said pointing. "You'll see a wee door marked 'Gents.' You can't miss it."

I walked along the narrow hall and pushed the door. One bare bulb, no brighter than a baby's nightlight, lit the room. I could barely make out where the toilet was. I stopped in my tracks, stunned by the odor. I knew right away that this is what I had smelled when I first came into Casey's the hour before. The urinal was so choked with cigarette butts that it had backed up and overflowed. I was gasping for air when I saw a dirt encrusted slit of a window high above the toilet. I stepped onto the seat, unlatched a hook, and forced the window frame open. I looked out to see a trash-strewn alley and pulled my head back inside. Enough light and air poured into the loo to make it almost tolerable.

When I was done, I decided to leave the window open, just in case I had to use the place again.

I went back and sat with Uncle Sean, who by then had two empty pint glasses and two full ones in front of him.

Just then a couple of guys came in with guitars. They settled into a nearby table, and Casey turned off the TVs. The boys hadn't even uncased their instruments when people began shouting names of songs. It got even louder when they actually began to play. And it wasn't just the two guys who sang. It was everyone. Even Casey and his son, probably even Casey's wife in the back room, belted out the songs.

I knew some of them as the songs Uncle Sean had sung back home—bawdy ballads and drinking ditties. But when they got into the patriotic ones, old songs about Irish heroes and ancient battles, that's when it got really loud. I knew some of them, too. They were the ones Mom walked out on back home, but here at Casey's nobody was walking out on these guys.

One song, "Skibbereen," was about the Potato Famine. It told how the English landlords, who were even more merciless than usual back in the 1840s, watched thousands of Irish people starve to death. All the while British ships hauled boatloads of Irish farm products back to England. Anyway, when the guy finished his song, he got a big hand. He then turned in his chair and faced Uncle Sean. His jaw dropped. He stood, bowed and said, "Sean Hanlon?"

"Aye, 'tis," Uncle said.

The man quickly held out his guitar to Uncle. A hush came over the crowd. As Uncle Sean took the instrument, he thanked the man and began to strum softly. When the pub got so still you could hear froth bubbling on the head of a Guinness, he began. Uncle's voice was soft, but full and rich:

"Come all ye young Rebels, and list' while I sing,
For the love of one's country is a terrible thing.
It banishes fear with the speed of a flame,
And it makes us all part of the patriot game."

That was the name of it, "The Patriot Game." It was an old, Rebel song. Everyone knew the lyrics, but they barely made a sound, mouthing the words as they sang along. They wanted to hear him, as if, by Sean Hanlon being with them that night and singing this song, a miracle would happen and all of Ireland finally would be united and free from English rule.

By the time Uncle was done, ladies were dabbing their cheeks with hankies, and men were wiping their eyes with the backs of their shirtsleeves. Uncle Sean returned the guitar to its owner. The man looked dazed, like he'd just been touched, blessed with Saint Patrick's staff and by Saint Paddy, himself.

This singing and passing the guitar went on for hours. I was glad I had taken that afternoon nap, because I didn't want to miss any of this. As I watched the people and listened to them sing and talk and laugh, I saw why Uncle Sean liked this place so much. I also realized that there was a lot more to my uncle than I had thought.

At a few minutes to eleven, Casey bellowed over the din, "Right, lads..." There was a rush to the bar, so I guessed it must have been time for last call.

Uncle nudged my arm and nodded to the door. "No last call for us," he said. "We need to get back. Lots to do tomorrow."

We left the pub and walked to Uncle's place. I pulled my shirt and pants off and, wearing only boxer shorts, covered myself with Uncle's coarse sheet and scratchy horse blanket. I settled onto the cot and closed my eyes. Sleep would not come easily as my mind raced through everything that had happened that day: the hassles at the airports, the dreams, and always the flashbacks of the planes smashing into the Twin Towers. I couldn't stop thinking about how Mom was killed in a flash and how Dad could have saved himself if only he had turned and run for the elevators while he could.

This first day in England was the beginning for all kinds of changes. I just hoped that tonight I wouldn't have one of my dreams. If I did, as thin as Uncle's walls were, I'd probably wake up half of London.

Chapter Nine

~~~~~~~

The next morning I woke up to see Uncle Sean standing in the kitchen. On the counter were plastic grocery bags with milk, bread, tomatoes, eggs, butter, and bacon. A dented tin kettle whistled on the gas stove. Uncle picked it up and poured boiling water into a chipped enamel teapot. "Hungry?" he asked, without looking my way.

"Starved," I said. "That was something else last night at the pub."

"Those are our mates," he said. "Our neighbors."

"You're more than a neighbor to them," I said. "They looked at you like you were some kind of hero."

"Och, no, I'm not the hero," Uncle Sean said, turning the eggs. "My only claim to that is through kinship. Your father was the hero. Brendan's name was revered all over Ireland."

"It sounds like he'd made his share of enemies," I said.

"Oh, aye, that he did," Uncle said. "All of them bloody Prods to be sure. But there wasn't a true son of Erin who didn't worship the ground Brendan Hanlon walked on. After the RUC gunned down our family and Brendan met your mum, all the fight went out of him. He said he was done with it. He had more to live for than to fight the IRA's battles. At first I figured he'd only been stung by Cupid's arrow. It would pass, so I thought, but it didn't. Still, everything he did for the Cause will be remembered in Ireland forever. And one thing is sure: The Irish never forget their heroes."

I nodded, but I also knew that, although my father was a

hero and patriot to some, to others, like my mother's family and other Irish Protestants, he was nothing of the sort. To them, he was a rabble-rousing, low-life terrorist, a person only to be feared and despised. His position among Irish countrymen depended upon which side of the fence they stood.

No matter how you cut it, before he met my mom, my dad did to her people the same sort of thing the al-Qaeda guys had done to America. And it wasn't a whole lot different from what Joey Cardle had done to me, magnified a thousand times—but the same idea. I hated to think of my dad as a terrorist, but it was hard to paint him any other way. I know he did what he did for a reason, and I know the reason, but killing innocent people, even in the name of the Cause, is still murder. I told myself that he finally woke up and changed his ways, but still...

I kept that thought to myself and switched the subject. "How long are we going to be here in London? Will I ever go back?"

"We'll be here a while, Michael," he said.

"What am I going to do about school? I can't skip forever."

"How'd you like to go here?" he asked.

"You mean, to an English school?"

He nodded.

"I don't know," I said. "Can I do that? I'm not a citizen or anything."

"You don't have to be," he said. "Well, at least not where I think you should go. To get in, all you need is some smarts, a little political pull and lots of cash. You've got all three."

I thought about that. I had always gotten good grades, but I didn't know about the other two. "I've got money?" I asked.

"Pots," Uncle Sean said. "After being on TV with President Bush, every church, Rotary Club and Chamber of Commerce in America from sea to shining sea, sent cash to help the victims' kids. Since both of your parents died, a huge amount was put in your name. That, along with all the money from selling your house, and you've got enough to get through any school in the world. Why not go to the best?"

"All right," I said, "but political pull?" I remembered Mr. Cardle and how he seemed to have influence over everyone in Eastham, even the police. "I didn't have any clout back home," I said. "For sure, I won't have any here."

"Oh, aye, that you do," Uncle Sean said. "The government bigwigs here will do cartwheels to show support for an American boy orphaned by what they call an unprovoked attack on the Western world."

"You think so?" I said. I knew I didn't have many choices. For sure I couldn't go back to Madison High. I wondered what it would be like to be thrown in with a bunch of British kids. How would I fit in? I remembered how hard it was moving from Brooklyn to Eastham and starting at North Middle. That was no piece of cake, but it turned out okay. I nodded and said, "I guess I could try."

"We'll start tomorrow with a call to the American Embassy," Uncle Sean said. "I'll tell them why you can't go back to your old school. And since I'm your legal guardian, and I only have a US visitor's card, you might have to stay here for a long time. I'll tell them, with all the publicity you've had, you need a place where you'll be safe." A loud truck rolled by as he added, "The best school I can think of is Bulwick."

"What?" I said. "Did you say, 'Bullwhip?' Are you sure? That doesn't sound very pleasant."

"No, I said Bulwick. It's spelled with a 'w' and pronounced 'bullick.' I don't know why the 'w' is even there, but that's how the bloody English do things. They make stupid rules and everyone else has to jump. Anyway, Bulwick's one of the most exclusive boys schools in all of Britain," Uncle said.

"All right, bullick," I said, saying it like Uncle did. I

remembered how Mom and Dad tried to sound American to fit in with other New Yorkers. It must have been hard, getting rid of their old accents, but if it was important for them, it should be important for me, too. "Bulwick," I said again, properly. Then I looked at Uncle Sean seriously. "Did you say it's a boys school? No girls?"

"Aye, lads only. Most are royals and sons of foreign big shots—ambassadors, people like that. It's very high-class. Eton would be okay, that's where Prince Charles' boys go. But that's in Windsor, miles away. Bulwick's right here in London, only forty minutes by bus. You could visit me as often as you'd like."

"Visit?" I said. "Couldn't I stay here with you and go to Bulwick? I mean, like you say, it's close enough."

"Oh, no," Uncle said. "If you go to Bulwick, you live at Bulwick. It's strictly a boarding school. Same for the teachers, groundskeepers, janitors, everyone. They all live right there."

"Sounds more like a prison camp," I said. "Does anyone ever get out?"

"Oh, aye," Uncle said. "I've read about it. The boys attend West End theatres; spend weekends in the Lake District, the Cotswolds, and places like that. They bounce all over England, the whole world. They have dinner-dances at girls' boarding schools, Wycombe Abbey and the like. You'll meet the fairest lasses in all of Britain. With your American accent, Michael, you'll have 'em eating out of the palm of your hand."

I laughed. "I don't have an accent. You have an accent. Casey has an accent. Everyone I've met has an accent. I'm the only normal-talking person around here."

"Oh, you have an accent, all right, and the girls will love it," Uncle Sean said. "So, what do you say?"

He made it sound pretty good. One thing was sure; I couldn't go back to America. "All right," I said. "I don't know how I'll fit in with the guys, them being all royal and everything, but I'll give it a try."

~

Uncle Sean was on the phone most of Monday, setting up meetings with British officials and people from the American Embassy. On Tuesday morning, he took me to Marks & Spencer, a big department store like Macy's. We both got new suits. That same afternoon, we met with the American Ambassador and the British Minister of Home Affairs. They thought I should go to a public school, which, in England means private. What they call a state school means public to us—go figure.

They said Bulwick was the best choice, but even with all their influence, it would still be hard to get in. After an hour of talking, the British guy shook my hand and said, "The best we can do is to arrange an appointment for you with the Bulwick School registrar, a Mr. Bassington. You're to meet with him Thursday morning at nine to take some tests. The rest will be up to you."

That night I had the first nightmare since I landed in England, and it must have been a doozy, a real screamer. When I woke up, someone was banging on the door. Uncle opened it. It was the police. Uncle let them in. I looked out and there was a big crowd of people standing around on the sidewalk. The cops put both of us in handcuffs and made us stand in the street while they went through Uncle's apartment to make sure no one had been murdered. When they didn't find any dead bodies, they looked me over to make sure I hadn't been beaten. Uncle told them who I was and they finally believed him.

After the cops left, the crowd broke up and went back to their places, all except for one girl. She was really cute, probably thirteen or fourteen. She came up to me and pointed across the street to where she lived. She said if Uncle ever did anything to me again to come over and knock on her door. Her parents would take me in. Her name was Felicity Brown. I liked her right away, maybe because she was the first London person I'd met who I could understand. She sounded a lot like my mom. Her accent was softer than Uncle's or anyone I had met at Casey's. I started to tell her that Uncle hadn't done anything to me, but then I figured, well, no sense slamming an open door. I went back inside and crawled onto my cot. I didn't have any more bad dreams that night but I couldn't get Felicity off my mind. I don't know about love at first sight, but I do believe in like at first sight. And I liked her a lot.

The next afternoon about four o'clock, Uncle said he had to go see someone. So while he was gone, I went across the street and knocked on Felicity's door. Her mom answered. She looked at me a little nervously, but then she recognized me and let me in. Felicity came in from her room, and when she saw me she broke into a huge smile. I can't say why, but I went from like to love right then.

We went for a walk and I found out that she had just turned fourteen, too, and was in a state school, which is like our public schools for regular kids. Her mom was real sick and her dad was out of work, so she was just taking vocational classes, hoping to get a job as soon as she could. She said she already had one job, but it was only on weekends. It wasn't enough to take care of her whole family. She was taking classes that would get her work in an office or something. What she really wanted was to become a doctor, but she knew that would be impossible.

I told her about why I'd had the nightmare the night before and that it wasn't anything Uncle had done to me at all. "I get this awful dream," I said, "and every time I do, I wake up screaming. See, the thing is, I blame my dad for not getting out of his building when he could."

"But he couldn't have known another plane was going to hit his place next, right?" Felicity said. "Put yourself in his place, Michael. He'd just watched his wife getting killed. He called your uncle so your uncle could tell you he was okay. He was thinking of you right up to the last second of his life. You've got to quit blaming him for dying. You're only feeling sorry for yourself."

I was about to argue that, but suddenly, it sank in. She was right. I was feeling sorry for myself, and maybe feeling guilty that I was alive and Mom and Dad weren't.

We walked and talked for over an hour until I started thinking about how hungry I was.

Felicity took my hand and said, "Let's nip into a McDonald's, my treat. I work there on the weekends. It's just ahead."

I looked up and down the street but didn't see any golden arches. Then she nudged me and said, "Right here." I looked to my right. I was almost standing on it. The place was hardly bigger than a closet. It had tiny golden arches painted on the door. We went in and she scored some burgers, fries and a Coke.

I walked her back to her place and got to Uncle's flat a few minutes after he had come home. He asked me where I'd been, and I told him I'd been across the street and had met a really cool girl. He asked me what her name was, and I told him, Felicity Brown.

He scrunched up his nose, like something smelled bad. "She's English, you know," he said.

"Maybe she is," I said. "So what? Besides, how do you know?"

He said, "It's an English name, Brown. And I'll bet she's a Prod, just like your mum. I just don't want you to get mixed up the way your father did. That's what happened to him. First pretty face that comes along and straight away you forget everything you've ever learned. I'm just saying you're traveling a slippery slope, that's all. I don't want you to get hurt."

And I said, "We just went for a walk. It's not like we're getting married." He didn't say anything more, but it got me to wondering about this new place. Does everyone get so caught up in names and religion that you can't even talk to anyone? Maybe the Troubles of the '70s never stopped. And maybe they're not just in Ireland. Maybe they're here in England, too.

Chapter Ten

B efore I knew it, Thursday morning came. Uncle Sean and I were on a bus, heading along Kilburn Road to a part of London called Bulwick-on-Thames. The day was cool, clear and sunny, and both of us looked pretty sharp in our new suits.

As we rode along, I got to thinking about all I had to go through just to get into a school. Back home I'd be assigned to one and that would be that. Here, I had already met a US ambassador, a British government minister and I was about to be examined by a school registrar. Except for my chance meeting with Felicity Brown, nothing much had gone my way. The bus came to a stop and Uncle stepped onto the sidewalk. I followed him and was soon staring at an ancient, three-story, orange brick building with stained-glass windows. The place looked like it might have been some rich guy's house, an earl or duke or something, some royal or other who had lived there ages ago.

A shiny brass plate had the words, "Bulwick School" printed on the wall. It was the first time I'd actually seen the name written out. Uncle was right. The "w" was there. Still, odd spellings and pronunciations shouldn't have surprised me, not after my "hay-um sammich" fiasco at Casey's.

The place didn't look like a school at all. And if this was all there was to it, it couldn't have had many students—thirty, tops.

We walked up the wide stone steps, and Uncle turned the fist-sized brass handle. The heavy door creaked opened. Across the street, a church bell began striking nine o'clock. I stepped inside. The front hall was all dark wood, from the floor to its sky-high ceiling. It was ultra-high class, nothing like Madison High, which was shiny and new but looked like a cookie cutter project compared to this. Bulwick School was clearly in another league, sort of like Eastham Community College would be to Harvard. I felt totally out of place. Just then the door clunked shut with a solid thud.

My eyes adjusted to the dark room. Uncle Sean put his hand on my shoulder and said, "Relax, Michael. It's no better than you deserve."

He could say that. He was just dropping me off. "Thanks," I said, "but I've got a feeling you're wrong. This is like a school for kings."

We walked along a wide hall and came to a door with another brass plate marked "Registrar." Uncle pushed it open and nudged me in.

I was facing a man who was about as snooty-looking as anyone I'd ever seen. He was staring back with a look that said, "What could this insignificant mongrel be doing here?" He gave a sniff and a weak smile as he stared back.

Uncle stepped forward. "I'm Sean Hanlon," he said firmly. "This is my nephew, Michael. We have an appointment to see a Mr. Bassington about Michael attending here."

"Good morning," the man said, his dour expression unchanged. "I am Mr. Bassington. I understand that your nephew, Michael, wishes to enroll in Bulwick School."

"Yes, sir," Uncle said curtly, like, "What are you, thick? Isn't that what I just said?"

I wondered the same thing and wanted to get this over with as quickly as I could. Everything Uncle had told me about the bloody English was probably true. Uncle replied as politely as he could, "As I believe you have been informed, Michael has had a rather rough go of it lately. The British and American officials suggest Bulwick would be the best place for him to continue his studies."

"Uh, yes, that may be so," Mr. Bassington said gravely, "but Bulwick School has extremely high standards. Its applicants must be thoroughly screened and approved before being admitted, regardless of circumstance. To begin with, we have yet to see any of Michael's scholastic records. In addition, a candidate must be able to prove his worth in social as well as academic achievement before being considered."

I looked at Uncle Sean. This was not going well. Uncle Sean glared at the man and said, "Maybe I didn't hear those English bigwigs and Yank blokes right. I believe they told us Michael could take the entrance tests like anyone else."

"You are quite correct," Mr. Bassington said stiffly. "I simply need to emphasize the school's strict admissions policy."

"I tip my hat to you for that," Uncle Sean said with a snort. "You have proven yourself worthy on that measure. Now, may we get on with it?"

"Very well," the man said, smiling pleasantly. He had either missed or ignored Uncle's sarcasm. "If young Mr. Hanlon is prepared, I will ask that you excuse us and we will proceed to the examination chamber. The tests, five in all, will require the better part of the day. You may return at four o'clock to collect your nephew. I will see to it that Michael will have tea and appropriate breaks. The Bulwick School admissions staff will assess Michael's work, after which, Headmaster Wilmot will make his final decision. Sir John will convey that result personally to you on Monday morning."

"Jolly good," Uncle Sean said with a fake British accent. He turned to me and whispered, "Show this English prig what Hanlon men are made of, Michael. Keep your wits about you. I'll be back at four."

With that, Uncle Sean turned and was gone. I stood alone with the school registrar.

The faintest smile formed on Mr. Bassington's thin lips as he ushered me from his office to a small room next door. He pointed to a straight-backed chair pulled up to a wide desk. Both were set before a tall window.

I sat down, pulled myself up to the desk and looked out at the grounds. Several boys my age and older were walking along flagstone paths through an enormous, perfectly landscaped campus. From where I sat I could see twenty or more buildings like the one I was in. I thought, *Those must be dorms and classrooms like they have at Ivy League schools, Yale and Harvard, places like that. The building I'm in is simply the school's administration office. This really is a school for kings.*

Several guys passed near my window smiling, laughing, and poking each other playfully. Something about them reminded me of my friends back home. I wondered what Roger, Scott and all my Count buddies were up to. I thought about the JV football team and how the games were going. My mind flashed to Mom and Dad. I watched the Twin Towers collapse. Just then, I heard Mr. Bassington say, "Is anything amiss?"

I glanced down and saw a drop of water on the desk in front of me.

I hated when this happened. I didn't want Bassington to think I was a wimp. I ran my hand over the moisture without looking up. "Uh, no, sir," I said. He was holding a white envelope under my nose. I reached for the test.

"This is your mathematics examination," he said. "I will return in one hour, the allotted time for its completion." He glanced at the wall where a large clock read 9:30. "You will then be given five minutes to move about before commencing the English literature portion of your day's tests. After that I will take you to lunch and show you a bit of the grounds. We are very proud of our school and would like you to see some of it before you leave."

The "before you leave" part seemed to mean "forever." I

was beginning to hope that it would be forever. None of this high-class stuff seemed right for me. I had half a notion to tell him to bag it right then, that he could keep his uppity school to himself. Then I remembered how hard Uncle had worked to get me here, how he told me to show this guy what Hanlon men can do. I took the envelope and tore it open.

He said, "After lunch, you will sit for the geography, sciences and history portions of the entrance requirements, whereupon it will be time for your uncle to return."

"Yes, sir," I said. His tone made me think the Bulwick School brass was simply going through the motions and following British State Department's orders. They had no intention of letting me in. I was wasting my time.

He handed me a pencil, a bottle of water and a crystal drinking glass. Etched into each was the Bulwick School crest, which had a lion rearing up on its hind legs. It looked like it was about to jump a fence and run away. I wanted to do the same.

"Will there be anything else?" Mr. Bassington asked.

I shook my head. "No, sir," I said.

"If you should need me, I'll be in the next room," he added. The massive door clunked behind him.

For a minute I felt like I had on 9/11, sitting in the media center at Madison High. All the other kids had gone home on buses or been picked up by their parents. Once again, I was alone. My stomach knotted, and I wanted to crawl into a hole. But then I remembered what Uncle had said about Hanlon men and picked up the pencil.

The questions went quickly from simple arithmetic to advanced algebra. It went on with a few geometry problems and finished with a trig question. I was glad my parents had made me take the college prep math programs in school rather than the regular classes. Mom and Dad told me to always challenge myself. If I didn't, I'd never know what I could really do, whether it was in school or sports or anything. Besides, math made sense to me. Its rules stayed the same no matter where you were, not like English.

When I finished the test, I looked at the clock and saw I had a few minutes to spare. I checked my answers, put the sheets in the envelope and sat back in my chair. I stared out the window and watched some guys kicking a soccer ball around on the grounds. I wanted to be out there with them. Then I remembered who they were: sons of royalty, rich kids. I didn't see any greasers, no Joey Cardles, but that didn't mean there weren't any jerks, either. I wondered if I would ever fit in.

Mr. Bassington knocked on the door and came in. He gave me an odd look, like he was surprised that I wasn't bent over my desk, frantically erasing an answer and scribbling another on the paper. I handed him the envelope.

"You decided not to take the exam?" he asked.

I answered, "No, sir. It just wasn't that hard. I finished a while ago."

He nodded slowly. "Very well," he said. "You have five minutes before your next test. Is there anything you need?"

"Just one thing, sir," I said. "Where's the loo?"

He gasped and said, "The loo?" His eyes were wide in shock. "Perhaps you mean the Gents or the Lavatory?"

The term Uncle had used that first night at Casey's was evidently not the one spoken by proper English gentlemen. "Uh, yeah, right. I mean, 'Yes, sir,'" I said.

"You will find the requested room down the corridor and clearly marked," Mr. Bassington said with a sniff. "I trust you will find its accommodations acceptable."

I went down the hall and, compared to Casey's, found it quite acceptable. I got back to Mr. Bassington's exam room with a minute to spare.

The registrar handed me the next envelope and I began.

73

Chapter Eleven

This one, the English Lit test, was a lot trickier. Back home we studied mostly American writers with a few British ones thrown in, but, all in all, I thought I did okay.

When the second hour was up, Mr. Bassington came back into the room. He still looked like a stuffed shirt, but he seemed friendlier. He said with a smile, "Right, let's meet some chaps at the dining hall. Are you hungry? I suppose that's a silly question. You're a fourteen-year-old lad. Of course you're hungry."

Actually, I was hungry, but what I really wanted was to find out what kind of guys went here. Were they all snobby like Mr. Bassington? Old folks in America can be like that, too. We hiked about fifty yards along a stone path to a place called, Admiral Nelson Dining Hall.

Just inside the door was a large notice board with sign-up sheets for fencing, rugby, chess and a dozen other clubs tacked all over it. Beyond that was an enormous open room with rows and rows of tables set up with hundreds of straight-back, wooden chairs.

"We're a bit early," Mr. Bassington said, "but in ten minutes' time the room will be filled with boys. I'll find a few Fourth Formers and introduce you."

"Fourth Formers?" I asked.

"Oh, that's right," Mr. Bassington said. "I believe in America they'd be called either eighth- or ninth-graders, boys with four to five years before entering university. Our school begins with the Lower Fourth Form, boys who are thirteen years old going on fourteen. The next year is the Upper Fourth Form for fourteen- to fifteen-year-old boys. I believe you are within that first age group?"

"Yes, sir, just turned fourteen," I said.

"Well, I checked your first exam, and if you score as well in the other spheres of study as you did in the maths, which is also my area of expertise, there may be a place for you here," Mr. Bassington said pleasantly. "I must say I am surprised by your aptitude. I had not expected such excellence from an American boy with only a state school education. Usually, only top scholars from the most elite preparatory schools produce such proficiency."

"So, I did okay?" I asked.

"Your answers were all correct," he said. "Still, we base entrance not only upon academic measures but also other civic and social skills. We consider how your experience at Bulwick School will benefit society after you leave."

Wow, that's a lot to put on a kid, I thought.

Just then, three boys, one black and two white, pushed open the cafeteria door. They were talking and laughing as they came in. The next thing I noticed was that each guy was wearing the funniest hat I'd ever seen. It was a flat-topped silk thing. I tried not to laugh, but I couldn't help it.

Then I saw the rest of their clothes. Each wore identical blue blazers, blue sweaters, black-and-red-striped ties, white shirts, gray flannel slacks, and shiny black dress shoes. They looked like junior Wall Street executives. With a get-up like that, none of them would have made it through the front door at Madison High, not without one of Joey Cardle's Demons ripping him apart.

"Gentlemen," Mr. Bassington said, getting their attention.

They turned and walked toward us. Except for the clothes, each looked as different as any three guys my age could be.

The first was tall and handsome. He had curly, blond hair

and struck me as the arrogant, snob type. Still, he seemed strong and athletic. My conclusion: He was good at sports, rich, and stuck on himself.

The second kid was very black-skinned, about my size, wore tiny glasses and was carrying an enormous book bag. He was the only one who smiled as he came toward us. I pegged him as the smartest of the three and the most friendly.

The last kid was short and pudgy, a total nerd if ever there was one. He wore thick, dorky, wire-rimmed glasses and looked totally out of place with the other two. For sure, he would be the last one picked in a playground game or anything else. Still, here he was with the other two, probably a desperate hanger-on. He eyed me nervously, like I might be some sort of threat to his place with the other guys.

I knew all this in about two seconds. I smiled warily and nodded to each of them.

"This is Michael Hanlon," Mr. Bassington said. "Michael has just arrived from the United States and is hoping to enroll here. I would appreciate it if you would be so kind as to show him through the cafeteria queue and then invite him to join you for lunch at your table."

"Of course," the black kid said, speaking for all three. The other two just looked me over.

"Thank you, gentlemen," Mr. Bassington said. "Now, if you will excuse me, I have an appointment." He faced me and said, "Michael, please return by half past twelve to continue your exams." He added, "Of course, there will be no charge for your meal."

I nodded to Mr. Bassington and watched as he walked away. I turned to the three guys, not feeling very comfortable with the short introduction.

"Nice to meet you, Michael," the tall, blond-haired kid said, smiling eagerly. He stuck his hand out to me. This was the one I guessed was the least friendly. I was wrong about him right away. "I'm Alfred Noyes, 'Alf' to my friends," he said.

Back when I was a kid, Mom told me it was important, when you're meeting someone, to remember his name. She said a person's name is the sweetest sound he can hear, so if you can remember it and call him by name, it'll show you respect him. She taught me a trick of how to do it.

"First," she said, "listen to the name when you're being introduced. Then, pick out something about the kid, a zit, funny teeth, anything, and match it up to the name. Then, make the connection huge. Like say, a guy's name is Erik. First, put 'Erik' with 'ear ache,' and then stare at his ear and pretend it's throbbing–red with pain. Then, next time you meet him, you'll see his ear and think, 'ear ache.' After a while, you forget the 'ear ache' thing and just remember the name."

So I got in the habit of doing that, and it worked, pretty much. I saw this big, athletic-looking kid and put "Alfred" with "Athlete." Whether he really was a jock or not, he looked like one. I pictured him in a shining white soccer uniform with dazzling white shoes, and "Alfred-the-Athlete" he became. I shook his hand. It was warm and friendly.

"It's not easy, entering a school after the term has begun," Alfred-the-Athlete said, "but there are lots of good lads here. The three of us live in Weatherby House, but no matter where you're put, you'll find that everyone will help you get on."

Then the black kid spoke up. "My name is Terrence Bonuku," he said. "I have only recently arrived to this country myself. My father is Zimbabwe's ambassador to Great Britain, so I know what it is to be the new chap in school." He spoke with perfect English diction. You would have thought he was a five-generation Londoner. "What Alfred is saying is true," he added. "Everyone here is very helpful to newcomers."

I did my name trick and pictured him as a college professor. Right away he became, "Terrence-the-Teacher." He was the smartest-looking person I'd ever seen. Anyway, he was next to shake my hand. He stared at me with a quizzical look, like he was trying to put my face with something he'd remembered. He said slowly, "Michael Hanlon, that sounds familiar. Might you be from New York City, something to do with the 9/11 attack?"

I nodded. "Yeah," I said. "Both of my parents were killed. I've come here to live with my uncle."

I glanced from face to face. They all stared at me. Several moments of awkward silence followed.

Then the third kid, the nerdy short one, shoved his pudgy pink hand out to me. He said somberly, "Hi, Michael. My name is Walter Tootlington, 'Tootles' for short."

I decided I didn't need a word trick for him. Tootles suited him just fine.

"You've had a rough go of it lately," Tootles said, "but you can count on us to help you get on with the others." He hesitated a moment as he flexed his shoulders and neck like boxers do in the center of a ring before a fight. Then he continued with a toss of his head, "If any Sixth Former comes along and gives you trouble, just tell him he'll have to answer to Tootles."

At that, the other two boys broke into an uncontrolled belly laugh, and so did I. Tootles pulled a handkerchief from his blazer pocket, took off his glasses and wiped them slowly. He winked at me, smiling at the effect his outlandish statement had made, like together we had just pulled one over on the two other guys. I felt like I was already a full-fledged partner of his comedy team. Any doubts I had about associating with this chubby little guy vanished in a heartbeat.

"Michael, you'll have to excuse our class joker," Alfred-the-Athlete said, still grinning. "Tootles is hopeless. On the first day of school, some Fifth Formers took him to the grove to give him a proper flogging. By the time they'd gotten there, he had them laughing so hard that none of them could lay a hand on his ever-so-deserving, smart aleck bum. I'm afraid we're stuck with

Tootles just the way he is. Actually, what he says is true. You'll find that you are as welcome here as if you were royalty."

"As you will find some of your fellow classmates to be," Terrence-the-Teacher said. "Mind you, I'm not one of them, royal that is, but you wouldn't have to shake any of our school's eleven boarding houses very hard without one or two blue-bloods falling out. Alfred, here," he nodded to the blond-haired kid, "he's a royal, but he's so far down the list he barely knows it himself. He pretends he's not one at all, but he is. Still, there are some chaps you'll meet who might rise to a position in the high court one day."

"Truth be known," Tootles said, "that's why everyone gets along so well. No one wants to cheese off a bloke who might, forty years on, point a long boney finger down at him and say, 'I remember you, you miserable slug. You peached on me back at Bulwick School.' And then he turns to a seven-foot tall brute wearing a black hood and holding a double-bladed axe, and says, 'Off with his head.'" Tootles turned from me and looked at Terrence and Alfred, who were trying to hold their sides. "All right, laugh if you will, but it happens. Look it up."

"I see what you mean," I said grinning. I was amazed how quickly the three had welcomed me into their group.

"I should caution you, however," Alfred-the-Athlete said seriously, "all that doesn't mean that we don't compete, because we do. You won't find harder-fought battles anywhere, whether they're on a rugby pitch or an English composition paper. We earned the right to come here by working hard in our previous schools. It's a privilege to be called a Bulwickian, and we all know it."

"Well, it's not for sure I'll get in," I said. "I'm just taking the entrance exams. I had two this morning and there'll be three more after lunch. I got the feeling my chances are pretty slim, so I'm not counting on much."

Chapter Twelve

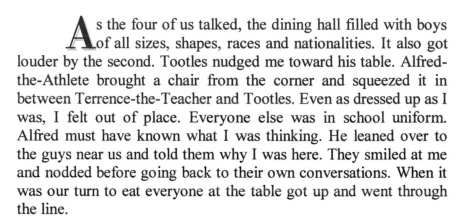

As the four of us talked, the dining hall filled with boys of all sizes, shapes, races and nationalities. It also got louder by the second. Tootles nudged me toward his table. Alfred-the-Athlete brought a chair from the corner and squeezed it in between Terrence-the-Teacher and Tootles. Even as dressed up as I was, I felt out of place. Everyone else was in school uniform. Alfred must have known what I was thinking. He leaned over to the guys near us and told them why I was here. They smiled at me and nodded before going back to their own conversations. When it was our turn to eat everyone at the table got up and went through the line.

I don't remember what I got or even eating it. I do remember how easily I fit in with Alfred, Terrence and especially Tootles.

After a while, Alfred looked at his watch and said, "It's twenty-five past twelve. You won't want to keep Mr. Bassington waiting."

"That's right," Tootles said. "It wouldn't do to set him off. If you hadn't noticed, our registrar is always a bit on edge. He feels he must look to be in charge, and since it's clear he's not, it puts him in a bit of a frazzle."

"Yeah, that's what I thought, too," I said. "He's seems sort of..." At that I couldn't think of the right word.

"Stodgy?" Alfred-the-Athlete said with a laugh.

"Yeah," I said.

"You're spot on," Tootles said. "That's one thing His

Lordship, Sir Starchface, has—plenty of, stodge. Check it out, that's his picture in the dictionary next to the word. Still, he's all right, in small doses."

I stood and waved to my three new friends and hurried out the way I'd come. When I got back to the main building, Sir Starchface was there waiting for me. I smiled as I thought of the nickname Tootles had hung on him. He handed me the next test and I went into the exam room.

By four o'clock, I'd finished the history test, my last exam. I tried not to show it, but I was dead tired. I handed the envelope to Mr. Bassington, and he led me down a long, dark hall.

On the door a shiny brass plate read, "Headmaster." Mr. Bassington ushered me in. The first person I saw was Uncle Sean, and he was looking extremely ill at ease. I turned and saw why. He was facing a man whose demeanor was even more cheerless than Mr. Bassington's. This guy looked like he'd been carved from the trunk of an old oak tree. His mouth was puckered like he'd been eating lemons for about a week. Mr. Bassington handed the man my exam folders, bowed and left the room.

"Michael, I am Sir John Wilmot, the Bulwick School headmaster," the tall, white-haired man said. The words came out of his head like a recording. I watched carefully. His lips did not move.

I used my name trick for "Wilmot" and came up with "Will Not," as in "He 'Will Not' let me into Bulwick School." But the more I looked, the more I thought, *For a block of wood, he has a decent smile.* I was probably wrong about him like I'd been about Alfred, Tootles and Terrence, and maybe Bassington, too. First impressions, which is what prejudice is, is a natural thing. It's not a good natural thing and not a very reliable yardstick, but it is human nature. Once someone makes a first impression, it sticks for a long time. I suddenly wondered what the others, Wilmot, Bassington, even Tootles, had thought about me.

"I am aware of the unusual circumstances under which you are requesting admission to our school," Mr. Will-not said. "I cannot promise that you will become enrolled here. In point of fact, our fourth form roster is completely filled at this time. In the unlikely event that an opening should arise, it would be patently unfair to the hundreds of boys who applied years in advance but did not place well on their exams, to allow you in—even if you meet our rigid standards. I do hope your scores prove you worthy, but given your previous educational experience, state-supported American schools and so on, I would not get my hopes too high. If that is the case, there are many other fine institutions in the London area where you might be more comfortable, both socially as well as academically."

I looked at Uncle Sean. His jaw tightened. The "social" reference, referring to my Irish name and its heritage, seemed to tip the scale. I remembered how Uncle had blown his stack with Dad back home, and how, when he got his dander up, he could singe the air. I knew what was coming. There was nothing I could do to stop it.

"It sounds a bit like a kiss-off to me," Uncle Sean said, his eyes burrowing into the headmaster's. "Suppose you keep your patronizing speech to yourself until you check Michael's scores. I'd hate to see such a fine man as yourself eat such high falutin' words."

I looked at Uncle Sean in disbelief. What little chance I had of getting into Bulwick School just went down the drain like tissue in a toilet.

The headmaster straightened his back and returned Uncle's stare. "Yes, well, that will remain to be seen," Mr. Will-not said abruptly. "My staff will review Michael's papers thoroughly. They will make their report, and I will announce my decision at 10 a.m. Monday. You will be so kind as to arrive at the appointed time. Good day."

Sir John stared at Uncle with a stern look of dismissal. He was done with us.

Uncle Sean grabbed my arm, turned and stalked out of the office. I practically had to run to keep up. We hurried down the long hallway and out the front door. When we got to the street, I said, "Uncle Sean, why did you say that?"

"That stuffed shirt just made my blood boil," he said. "They're all alike, every English bloke I've ever met treats us Irish like trash. Did you hear him? I'll bet every boy here is just like he is, pompous and arrogant."

"No, Uncle, they aren't," I said. "I sat with three of them at lunch. They were about the nicest guys I've ever met. I really want to come here."

Uncle Sean stopped, turned and stared at me. "You can't be serious," he said.

"Yeah," I said. "They're really good guys."

Uncle Sean turned away and muttered, "Well, I sure didn't read that from your face when Mr. Bassington led you into Sir John's office. You looked like you'd just been run through a meat grinder and squeezed into a tub like so much blood sausage."

"The tests were hard, but not impossible," I said. "I was tired, that's all."

"Well, I hope you did well enough to make up for my little fit of pique," Uncle said.

"Yeah, me too," I said.

We went across the street to the bus stand and waited. *Oh, well,* I thought, *like the man said, there are plenty of other schools around.*

But I liked this one.

We took the Kilburn Road bus back to Uncle's place. As

we went inside, he said, "Let's go to Casey's. I'm not up to fixing tea."

He changed his clothes and we went to the same hole-in-the-wall pub we'd gone to on my first night in London. Again, we were welcomed with open arms, or I should say, Uncle was. Dressed like I was, all duded up, I could feel everyone staring at me.

Then Casey recognized me. He laughed and said to Uncle, "What have we here, a newly appointed earl?"

"Don't start on me, Casey," Uncle said. "It's been a rough day. Michael took a whole battery of tests to get into a first-class school, and I'm afraid I mucked it up for him."

"No, I'm sure you didn't, now," Casey said. "What school was that?"

"Bulwick," Uncle answered "Get me a Guinness and a lemon mineral for the boy." He turned to me. "Lemon all right?"

I nodded.

"Bulwick School?" a gruff-looking man in a worn tweed jacket snorted. "What made yeh think a' Bulwick? Why not Eton—er straight off t' Oxford?" he added with an unpleasant guffaw.

"'Tis so, Sean," another man said. "Bulwick's just fer uppity little lords and sons a' foreign kings. That's all what goes there. They'll turn a good Irish lad to nothin' but trouble, sure they will."

An old woman in a shabby housedress downed the last swig of her half pint and said, "Sure and he'll be orderin' his poor uncle around soon enough. Us too, like as not." She tapped a cigarette out of a small box, lit it and said to Casey, "Be a good boy and draw yer sister another 'alf."

"Sure, Maggie," Casey said. He took her glass and filled it. Then he turned to me, smiled and said with his phony Texas drawl, "And I suppose you'll be havin' a plate a' hay-um sammiches for tea?" This brought a laugh from everyone at the bar.

After my miserable meeting with Mr. Will-not, it felt good to be with Casey and his crowd. I answered him with my own fake drawl, "Yer dang tootin', Casey. An' while you're at it, I'll have a sack a' them there patata chips."

Uncle just shook his head as everyone at the bar got into the act. Casey's kid, Liam, started rushing around taking orders for hay-um sammiches. He passed out bags of crisps to everyone in the whole place.

I watched the fun, even if it was at my expense. Uncle was right. These were our people. I belonged here. I didn't belong at Bulwick School. I wasted only one day finding out, first hand, how the English had treated the Irish for the past untold centuries. Still, I remembered how I had fit in with Terrence, Alfred and Tootles. Oh, well, I'd just have to chalk Bulwick School up to experience. It was probably for the better.

Later, a guy with a guitar came in and started singing Irish songs. Everyone, myself included, joined in. Some of the songs were funny. Some were serious and told how Irish kids worked for practically nothing in British factories. But like before, the best songs were the ones that told of Irish heroes who died trying to free Ireland from English tyrants.

The guitar started getting passed around and pretty soon it got to our table. Uncle Sean played "Boys from the County Cork." When he finished that, someone called out, "How about the 'Hay-um Sammich kid."

Everyone looked at me.

"Yeah," another yelled, "if he's a Hanlon, he must sing. How 'bout it, son?"

Everyone stared at me and cheered. I looked at Uncle Sean to see if he thought that would be a good idea. He nodded and said, "Go ahead, Michael. Play that one you do with those friends of yours, the song about the two blokes who go all over the place, work in fields, and then one of them dies. You know..."

"Ramblin' Boy?" I asked, wondering why he'd picked that one. "I know some Irish songs. I could do one of those."

Uncle Sean handed me the guitar and whispered, "Michael, you're better off doing an American song. Around here, until you know for certain who you're singing to and what your song is about, you can't do anything political. And here's something else: All Irish songs are political. That is, unless you're talking about Broadway tunes, like by Rodgers and Hammerstein. Those you can sing, because they're about as Irish as that O'Neal basketball player of yours, the Shaquille bloke. Look, I know it's very big in America to thumb your nose at authority by singing all sorts of protest songs, but here you can get yourself into some serious trouble, and mighty fast. If you so much as whistle an Orange tune at Casey's, my friends would haul you out by your heels and give you a good, old-fashioned butt whippin'."

"An Orange tune?" I asked.

"There, see?" Uncle Sean said, rolling his eyes. "You don't even know what I mean. I keep forgetting how American you are. Orange is for William of Orange, the Prod King of England. In 1690, he brought his army to Ireland and crushed our Rising at the River Boyne. He's a hero to the bloody Prods, but hated by any of us real Irishmen."

I didn't think I knew any Orange songs, but I sensed that anything related to that color carried with it some serious political baggage. I nodded, picked up the guitar and sang, "Ramblin' Boy."

The song is about these two guys, migrant workers, who go from farm to farm—Oklahoma or Kansas, places like that— looking for work. It's during the Depression, way back in the 1930s. They get jobs, work for a while, and then move on. One day one of them gets sick. Since they don't have any money, no doctor will come to help him. The sick one dies, and the other one cries over the only friend he ever had. When I was done, I got a big cheer. It had apparently struck a familiar note with Casey's crowd.

Maybe stories like that happened here, too. Anyway, they gave me a really nice hand. Even Casey liked it. Still, he wasn't so caught up that he didn't forget last call right at five to eleven.

As Uncle Sean and I were leaving, Casey said to me, "Bloody good job, son. Be sure to come back Saturday night. I've got a Belfast band coming. I'd like it if you could sing another of your songs."

Well, that got me going, Casey personally asking me to play. It wasn't like I'd just be there taking turns like everyone else. I started thinking about which song I should do.

Chapter Thirteen

I woke up that night with another screamer. Uncle got to me before anyone could call the cops, so it wasn't like the last time. Still, I couldn't get back to sleep, thinking about the planes ripping into the WTC and how Mom and Dad had been killed. I thought about what Felicity said, blaming Dad for dying on me and how I was just feeling sorry for myself. She was probably right. Anyway, I sat on my cot for an hour, not wanting to put my head down, afraid the dream would come back.

Then I started wondering about going to another school. The more I thought about Bulwick and the guys I'd met, the sorrier I was about how it turned out. Sir Will-Not wouldn't make it official until Monday, but there was no doubt what he'd say.

Next morning when Uncle had gotten out of bed I asked him, "Aren't there any schools around here that have mostly normal kids, maybe with some Americans?"

"Sure, sure, Michael," Uncle Sean said. "And we'll look into them, but I know you're keen on Bulwick. I'm not going to chuck it in until we hear it from that English bloke himself. I'm just sorry I blew up at him, but it's so cussed hard to keep a civil tongue with his kind. I've been thinking: I might know someone who can help, a Belfast man who knew your dad a long time ago. He lives near here, has some pull. Don't let it be a worry to you."

The part about "pull" should have been a red flag, but I wasn't thinking.

The next afternoon, Saturday, Uncle Sean took me to a rugby match. It was a big deal—London Irish versus Bristol. Uncle popped for the tickets and we walked into this big oval stadium. It was a perfect day, clear, cool and the air was charged, like for a Yale/Harvard or Army/Navy game. The place was jammed. Ten thousand people stood shoulder to shoulder.

The game hadn't even started and people were yelling these long, droning songs, which sounded like painful, monotonous groans. Nobody that I could see was leading it, no bouncing girls in short skirts or mascots with megaphones. The sound came from nowhere and everywhere at once. While the stadium shook, everyone was knocking down pint after pint of beer. It was amazing.

The game began and during the first half, between chugging Guinness and howling with the rest of the fans, Uncle Sean filled me in on the rules. The game was a little like American football but with more kick and less throw. Any throwing that was done had to be backwards, no forward passes allowed. The team with the ball had two ways to get it down the field. First, they could run it, which, like American football, usually got them only a few yards before getting tackled. The second way was to kick it, which was sort of like passing, except without much accuracy. That got the ball down the field but almost always into the other team's hands.

The game went back and forth in constant motion, offense to defense. The same players were on the field the whole time. Nobody wore helmets or pads, and it took a concussion or a broken leg for a guy to get a rest. Wherever you stood in the stands, you could hear the crashing of heads, the primal grunts and angry shouts. It was more like tag team wrestling with fifteen men to a side.

Another great thing was that the clock didn't stop after every single play like it does in American football. And there were no huddles or TV timeouts. It was nonstop action.

Before long, I started picturing myself as one of the small, quick ball carriers called backs. After the scrum, which is how the play starts, a back would get the ball from a forward and he'd run along behind the line of scrimmage. All the time he'd be looking for a hole in the defense. If he found a likely spot, he'd cut up field and head for the goal line.

More often though, several guys from the other team would close in and block the hole. So, just before being tackled, the guy with the ball would flip it to a teammate, who would try his luck. This would go on until the last back, the wing, got close to running out of bounds. He'd have to kick it downfield as far as he could, hoping one of his own guys could get it. If that happened, the guy who caught it would run straight to the goal line. But like I said, that hardly ever worked. Someone on the other team would get the ball and start for the opposite end of the field.

The whole thing was like a game we played at recess when I was a kid. It was called "football tag." The guy with the ball was "it," and everyone else tried to tackle him. Anyway, it was all against one, and the only rule was that the guy with the ball had to keep it for as long as he could. If he dropped it before getting tackled, everyone would think he was chicken. But if he held it too long, the big guys would catch him and drive him seriously into the ground. The smart thing for the guy with the ball to do was to figure out just the right time to "lose his grip" on it. One of the chasers would pick it up, and he'd be the new "it." That would go on until the recess bell rang and we'd go back into school, covered in mud and smelling like pigs.

Rugby was sort of like that only with goal posts, chalk lines and lots of people standing around in a stadium, chugging pints and screaming for blood.

At halftime, the home team, London Irish, was ahead by a few points and Uncle went to the loo. I didn't see him again until the match was almost over, but that was okay because I was really into the game. I knew I could play this sport. At least, with guys my age.

When Uncle and I got home, it was almost time to go to Casey's. Uncle got out Dad's guitar and said, "Michael, you may meet an important man there tonight."

"One of the guys in the band Casey was talking about?" I asked.

"No," he said. He looked at me seriously. "There's a gentleman who might be able to undo the harm I did at Bulwick School the other day. You know, with that Wilmot bloke, the headmaster."

"Really?" I said. "Who?"

"He's the Belfast man I told you about yesterday," Uncle said. "He's got a lot of influence around here. I got a word with him at halftime during the rugby match. I told him you were Brendan's son and that you were trying to get into Bulwick School. I know I shouldn't be the one to say this, but when you meet him, be on your best behavior. If he likes how you handle yourself, he may be able to help. Of course, we'll both owe him a very big favor."

I stiffened my back as he said this. The whole "Joey Cardle" thing jumped into my head. I remembered Dad telling me how once a spider gets you into his web, sooner or later you're going to be its meal. "Uncle," I said, "If it takes favors to get into Bulwick School, I don't want to go there. Honest."

Uncle Sean stared me in the eye and said, "Let me tell you something, Michael. Life is full of deals like this. It's not what you know, but who you know that gets you places. Sometimes you have to swallow a little pride. This man isn't likely to give you another chance. Do you remember the song about the preacher and the flood?"

"Sure," I said. It was one Roger, Brianna and I used to sing. It was about a preacher who lived in a house along the Mississippi. One day a big storm hits and rain comes down in buckets. The river floods and this preacher runs to his house, which is knee deep in water. So he climbs the stairs to the second floor. The rain keeps falling, the water keeps rising and the preacher keeps climbing higher and higher. Finally, the house starts floating down the river and the man ends up on the roof, holding on for dear life.

One by one, a rowboat, a Coast Guard cutter and a chopper come to save him, but each time, the preacher says, "No, no, no, the Lord will save me." Finally, the house sinks into the river and the preacher drowns. He goes up to heaven and when he meets the Lord, he says, "Lord, why didn't you save me?" And the Lord says, "What did you want? I sent you two boats and a helicopter."

It loses a bit in the telling, but that's the gist of the song.

Uncle said, "You know which song I mean?"

"Yeah," I said, "I know it. What about it?"

He said, "Don't be the preacher."

I got the message, but I still wasn't too thrilled about meeting this guy. On the one hand, he'd been a buddy with my dad, so I figured he'd be on my side. But on the other, as a kid, my dad wasn't exactly a saint. Probably, neither was this guy. My dad got smart, had seen the light and gotten out of Dodge. But his pal might have become a real lowlife.

"What's his name?" I asked, like that might give me a clue.

"Pearse Devlin," Uncle Sean said.

It didn't. "How will I know when he gets there? To Casey's, I mean."

"You'll know," Uncle answered.

That should have been my clue.

When we got to the pub, Casey saw me. He smiled and twanged loudly to his son, "Hey, Liam. The Ay-merican lad is here."

Instantly, Liam looked up and so did everyone else.

"Yahoo!" Liam whooped and began taking hay-um sammich and patata chip orders from everyone in the place. I noticed that nobody went so far as to ask for bottles of lemon mineral. Instead, they stuck with their pints of Guinness or drams of Tullamore Dew. They were willing to play their parts in this little charade, but only so far.

When the band got there, they went right into their Irish songs. After about an hour, they took a beer break. Casey walked over and asked me to play. I got Dad's trail guitar and went to the small stage.

I started "The Preacher and the Flood" and hadn't gotten much past the preacher getting to the second floor when the door to Casey's opened. A man walked in. He was dressed well enough, but he had a rough look about him. His bushy eyebrows were knotted into a frown. He reminded me of what Uncle had said about Dad during the Troubles, how he scowled all the time. Still, I couldn't picture my father being friends with this guy, even as boys.

As he walked through the crowd, the man's eyes flashed, taking in everything and every person there. People standing at the bar moved away, their expressions showing both fear and respect. He took a seat at a table, which had been left empty moments before by a guy who had shielded his face, disappeared in the crowd and slipped out the door.

This new guy nodded to Casey and then turned to me.

Casey filled a glass with whiskey and Liam rushed it to his table. The man picked it up and tossed half of it down in one swallow. He stared at me and wiped his chin with the back of his hairy left hand. He took another quick look about the room, and then his eyes settled on me.

For sure, this was the Belfast guy. Luckily, I knew the "Preacher" song well enough that I was able to get through it without sounding rattled. I finished and again got a big cheer, bigger than usual. I passed the guitar along to Uncle.

The Belfast man began to walk in our direction. Those in his path nearly fell over themselves, getting out of the way, parting like fishing boats for the *Queen Mary*. He came straight for us. As he did, Uncle got to his feet and nudged me to do the same.

"Mr. Devlin," Uncle Sean said, "I'd like you to meet my nephew, Michael, Brendan's son." He then turned to me, "Michael, this is Mr. Pearse Devlin."

I reached my hand to him. Mr. Devlin's palm was thick. His fingers hard and calloused. His grip snapped over mine like a bear trap. He stared threateningly into my eyes. Suddenly, he jerked me forward, pulling me off balance. Without another word, he turned to Uncle Sean and said, "I'll speak with Michael in the back room. Alone."

"Yes, sir," Uncle said, nodding and stepping aside.

I followed Mr. Devlin as he moved toward the bar. He lifted the hinged countertop and brushed Casey aside. He pushed open a narrow door to the back room. I looked at Uncle Sean, who nodded anxiously for me to follow.

I hurried to catch up and slipped into the office as Mr. Devlin was easing himself into a tall leather chair behind a desk. I stood there for a second before he said, "Go ahead, son, sit down."

There was a short stool in the corner. I pulled it up to the desk and sat. It was so low that I had to look way up at him. He towered over me like, if he had been a judge, he could have banished me to Siberia if he'd wanted.

"So, yeh wanna go to Bulwick School, do yeh?" he said with a hoarse, Godfather-like voice.

I answered, almost apologetically, "Well, that's where the British Home Office and the American Embassy think I should go."

His face clouded into a snarl. "Well, do yeh or don't yeh?" he growled.

I was taken aback by his tone, but I remembered Uncle's advice about the preacher song: This might be my only chance to get into Bulwick School. I held my tongue, but it got me mad, him grilling me like this. I tried not to sound upset, so I sat straight, stared him in the eye and said, "Yes, I believe I do."

He glowered even more fiercely and bellowed, "You believe you do? Look, boy, I knew your dad years ago and I'm sorry to hear of his passing, but if you don't know your mind, then you're no son of his. Now answer me straight. Do you want to go to Bulwick School or don't you? Is that clear enough?"

That did it. Blood rushed to my head. There was no turning back.

"Yes, sir," I said, returning his steely glare. "But if I make it, it will be on my own, not from any strings you or anyone else pull to get me there. Is that clear?"

I had just stepped over the line and lost my only chance with this Devlin character, but I didn't care. I wasn't going to be this spider's meal. If he didn't like my attitude, well, the feeling was mutual.

His scowl changed instantly to an almost pleasant smile. "By God, you are your father's son," he said. He leaned back in his chair. "All right, we'll see how you do without me, but if you need help, I'll be around."

He got up, moved past me to the door and was gone before I could stop shaking.

I walked out of the office, passed Casey behind the bar and worked my way through the crowd, which, surprisingly, parted for me almost like it had for Pearse Devlin. I found Uncle Sean just finishing a pint. He put down the jar, smiled and said, "Well, how'd it go? Is he going to get you in?"

"If I need his help, he'll see what he can do," I said. "We left it at that."

Chapter Fourteen

~~~

That Monday morning Uncle and I took the bus to Bulwick School and walked into the headmaster's office at ten sharp. Sir John Wilmot was standing at his desk, a tiny grin playing on his thin lips. I couldn't tell if was a mocking smirk or a real smile. I expected the worst—a sarcastic, anti-Irish insult and a swift boot out the door. Uncle had warned me that I should expect no better from an Englishman.

Instead, Sir John surprised me with an enthusiastic handshake. "Michael," he said, "I'm pleased to tell you that you scored extremely well in your examinations. Without fear of contradiction, you are academically equal to or above the level of any of our Lower Fourth Formers. I'm sure, with the help of our tutors, you will get along just fine. I would have telephoned you Saturday afternoon, but I had no number to reach you."

I glanced at Uncle. He had the same stunned look I knew I'd see if I looked in a mirror.

"Now," Sir John continued, "since the term has already begun, I am limited as to your room assignment. Quite unexpectedly, one vacancy has arisen in Weatherby House, which I would have thought the best fit for you anyway. If there is no objection, I will supply you with a list of necessities—clothing, shoes, sports gear and so on. All may be obtained at Sterns & Andrews, the haberdashers here at Bulwick-on-Thames. They have been fitting out Bulwick scholars for generations. They'll have you properly attired and back in time for me to introduce you to the Weatherby housemaster. You will commence classes immediately after lunch. Any questions?"

"Uh, no," I mumbled. "But this is kind of sudden. I didn't bring any of my stuff, you know, toothbrush, uh, pajamas."

Sir John smiled and said cheerily, "You'll find everything you need at Sterns & Andrews. The gentlemen there are prepared for such occasions. Now, if that is your only concern, I'll take you to the door and point you in the shop's direction. It's just a few minutes' walk from here. I'll ring them to let them know you are coming."

Uncle Sean and I just stared at each other. We followed Sir John as he walked quickly to the front door. He opened it and looked down the street to a small shopping district.

"There you are. It is among those buildings on the right," he said, pointing. "You can't miss it. Remember, Sterns & Andrews. Hurry along now. I'll meet you back here by eleven." He looked at Uncle Sean. "We'll stop by the business office afterward. Did you bring the term's fees?" he asked, then added quickly, "No, of course not. You couldn't have known. Oh well, can't be helped. Just sorry Mr. Bassington didn't get your telephone number."

"Uh, right," Uncle Sean said. "I'll go to the bank this afternoon, square you up with a check tomorrow."

"That will be quite satisfactory," Sir John said pleasantly. "Since Michael's already behind the other boys in his class work, it wouldn't do to delay him further. You may post the money or bring it here at your convenience. Right," he said finally. "Hurry along now." The huge door clanked solidly behind us.

I looked at Uncle Scan. "Are you sure that was the same guy we saw last week?"

"Aye," he said, "but I'd not have believed it." He still looked stunned.

I stared at Uncle and asked, "You didn't say anything to your Belfast friend to get me in, did you? I told him I didn't want any favors."

"Not a word," Uncle said defensively. "Mr. Devlin did ask

me how you expected to pay for such an expensive school. I told him about what you'd gotten for selling your parent's house and the money from American charities. If I hadn't told him that much, he'd have thought I was mad to even think of getting you in here."

"That's it?" I said.

"I swear," Uncle Sean said. "Besides, you heard what Wilmot said. By Saturday afternoon you'd already been accepted. He just couldn't phone us."

"Yeah, I guess," I said. "All right, let's get up to that store."

We started along the street. A little shopping district, maybe a dozen stores, stood just a few hundred yards away. In two minutes' time I saw a wooden sign hanging from a shop's doorway. It read, "Sterns & Andrews, Serving British Royalty since 1666."

Two men in suits met us as we walked in. A third guy with a well-worn tape measure dangling from around his neck was sizing me up.

"Mr. Hanlon?" the first man asked, smiling eagerly.

"Yes, sir," I nodded.

"A new Bulwickian I take it," he added.

I guessed what he meant, and said, "Yes, sir."

"We've been expecting you," he said. "Sir John rang a few minutes ago and asked that we do our best to serve you quickly."

"It is our pleasure to welcome you to our establishment," the second man said. "Did Headmaster Wilmot say where you'd be rooming?"

"I think he called it Weatherby House," I said.

"Ah, yes. Top drawer," he said. "Loads of tradition. We have your tie and sports colors all in stock."

The three worked together, gathering clothes, measuring and fitting me. In no time, I had everything from the shiny black shoes to the funny silk hat. It was the same outfit I had seen the three boys wearing the week before at lunch. Then the salesmen piled on loads of other stuff: a tennis sweater, rugby shirts, pajamas, a tank top and swimming trunks. Everything had red and black stripes somewhere on them. The men gathered pairs of sneakers, rugby boots and house slippers. It all went into a big trunk.

"I'm going to need all this?" I said to the first man.

"This will do for now," he answered.

"Will your classes commence soon?" the other asked.

"Mr. Wilmot wanted me back by eleven," I said. "I guess I start then."

"Ah, yes. Since that is the case, may I suggest you return in proper classroom attire?"

I nodded, and he set out the regulation uniform. I went to the changing room and put on the white dress shirt, charcoal slacks, blue sweater and black shoes. I struggled with the red-and-black striped tie, finally getting a halfway decent knot. I finished it off by putting on the goofy-looking silk hat.

I stepped out of the dressing room, and Uncle Sean stared at me with an odd expression. "I never thought I'd see a Hanlon looking so British," he said.

"This was your idea, remember?"

"Aye, and soon you may do more for the Cause than any Hanlon before you."

I wondered what he meant by that. The thought of the spider and the fly with Pearse Devlin flashed through my head, but before I could say anything, Uncle had turned away and was speaking to the salesman.

When he turned to me, I asked him, "How much is all this going to cost?"

"The school or just the clothes?"

"Yeah, well, the whole package," I said.

"Bulwick School, for one year, runs about 25,000 pounds, roughly forty-thousand dollars," Uncle Sean said. "The clothes are extra."

"You're kidding!" I said. "I don't have that."

"Oh, aye. That you do," he said. "Your dad's house sold for a small fortune, and the American charities were very generous."

As we talked, the two salesmen went through the store and filled a duffel bag with socks, toothpaste, hairbrush, deodorant— all kinds of everyday stuff. They handed the bag to me and told me the trunk would be delivered within an hour. Uncle and I turned and walked back to the school. We met Sir John in his office at eleven o'clock.

"Jolly good," Mr. Wilmot said, looking me over. "I told you they would be prompt. Is everything being delivered to Weatherby House?"

"Yes, sir," I said.

Sir John turned to my uncle. He reached his hand to Uncle Sean and said, "Right. I believe Michael is ready to meet his new school chums. I'll take him over and introduce him to his housemaster. So Mr. Hanlon, until we meet again, good day."

Uncle Sean shook Sir John's hand, turned to me and said, "All the best, Michael. I'll talk to you soon." In seconds he had left by the High Street door.

Once again, I was on my own. This was happening a lot lately, and every time it did, it came suddenly. This one turned out okay, but I wondered how the next would go.

"Right," Sir John said. "Off we go."

I picked up my new duffel bag and followed Mr. Wilmot into the bright, late-September morning. As we crossed the High

Street, directly in front of us stood an ancient, four-story, orange-brick building with turrets, ivy-covered walls and wavy, leaded-glass windows. It looked like a castle. We climbed the wide stone steps and went inside. Even the vestibule was enormous.

"This is your new home, Michael," Sir John said. "Grand, isn't it? Weatherby House is the second oldest residence at Bulwick School. It was built in 1790 and is named for Harry Weatherby and his son, Ben. As housemasters, they held authority all the way from 1806 until 1863. Weatherby House has a most distinguished list of old boys."

"Old boys?" I asked. It sounded like a put-down, but coming from Sir John, it was probably just the opposite, a term of high respect.

"Weatherby old boys, former Bulwick scholars who resided here," he said. "Many went on to make their marks in the world, not the least of which is Lord Featherston," he added importantly.

"I'm sorry," I said. "Lord who?"

"Lord Featherston," Sir John repeated, turning to face me. "Ah, but of course, as an American you might not be familiar with the name. Here he's as well-known as your Thomas Jefferson or John Adams. Featherston was the British Prime Minister. Served as such, off and on, during the nineteenth century."

I muttered a weak apology for my ignorance.

"Another Weatherby old boy is Lord Bowersox, the author," Sir John cruised on. "I'm sure you've heard of him. He was one of your answers on the English Literature exam. George lived here from 1801 to 1805. Interesting lad, even then. Fact is, you'll be living in the same room he had in his Shell year."

Before I could ask what that meant, Sir John ushered me into the cavernous living room. It had huge, overstuffed couches and long study tables. The walls were crammed with portraits, no doubt of famous old boys. He pressed a brass button, and from deep within the walls of the building, a bell rang.

From down a long hall, a thin, balding man in his late thirties came toward us. When he saw Mr. Wilmot, he smiled and said eagerly, "Sir John." Then he noticed me and smiled even more broadly. "And you must be my new charge. Sir John and Mr. Bassington have told me about you. You scored extremely well on your entrance exams. We will be expecting great things from you."

I nodded to him, my ears flushing from the praise.

"You are correct, Mr. Epping," Sir John said. "This is Michael Hanlon." Sir John turned to me and said, "Michael, this is Mr. Epping, Weatherby's housemaster." He looked at Mr. Epping again and said, "As you know, Michael is a Shell and will be residing here. Please be so good as to give him his timetable and acquaint him with other members of Weatherby House."

"Indeed, I shall, sir," Mr. Epping said with a slight bow.

Sir John Wilmot looked again at me and offered his hand, "Michael, I'm very pleased to have you here at Bulwick School. I'm sure you will get on famously. Excuse me now. I must be getting along." At this, he turned and left Weatherby House by its front door.

I looked at Mr. Epping. He smiled and said, "Well, let's get started, Michael. Have you ever been a student at a boarding school before?"

"No, sir," I said. "I've always just lived at home and gone to the local schools."

"Well, that alone will make a difference in your academic routine. As the housemaster, I'm here to assist each boy, whatever his background, and ensure that all his needs are met. Beside myself there are several other people here to benefit your stay. You shall have a tutor for class work, an older boy or 'shepherd' to aid with social adjustment, and so on. But remember: If you have any questions or problems, I'm always at your service."

I said to Mr. Epping, "Mr. Wilmot says I'm a 'Shell.' What's that?"

"Ah, yes," he said, thoughtfully. "Right. A Shell is a Bulwick expression that simply means that you are enrolled in our first-year curriculum, which is also known as the Lower Fourth Form. The term Shell comes from an earlier practice here of having all the first-year students eat their meals together in a separate area of the old dining hall. The ceiling there was shaped like an oyster shell, and thus the term began. And by old, I mean hundreds of years ago. Bulwick School was officially founded in 1590, but its roots go back closer to King Arthur's time than Queen Elizabeth's. And I do mean the first Queen Elizabeth, not the current one. After a boy's first year, he was removed from the shell and ate with the older boys in the main refectory. Thus, for his second year, he was referred to as a Remove. The terms Shell and Remove stuck and are still used today for our first and second year boys."

I must have looked confused because Mr. Epping added, "Those are the two Fourth Form years, Lower and Upper. Then there is the Fifth Form year and two Sixth Form years. Again, Lower and Upper. After graduation, off you go to university, Oxford or Cambridge, more than likely. But as a Bulwick scholar, the doors to any university in the world will be open to you."

"Okay," I said. I liked him right away. He was more like a big brother than a house father.

"I'm afraid there are lots of expressions here that might be confusing, especially to an American. Bulwick School has boys from all over the world, but none right now from the United States," he said. "If someone uses a term that you don't understand, just ask. That's the only way you'll learn."

He smiled, as if waiting to see if I understood. I nodded.

"Right," he said, "I'll show you up to your room. You will have a roommate, another Shell, whom you will meet this afternoon. I'm sure you don't know him, since you've come so recently from America. His name is Walter Tootlington."

I stared at the housemaster. "Tootles?" I asked.

Mr. Epping looked at me strangely. Finally he said, "That's either a very astute guess, or you and Mr. Tootlington have previously been introduced."

"We met last week," I said excitedly. "I had lunch with him and two other boys. It was the day I took the entrance exams."

"What a happy coincidence," Mr. Epping said. "So, you hit it off?"

"Yes, sir, right away," I said. "Same with the other two guys."

"And they would undoubtedly be Alfred Noyes, a tall, fair-haired, athletic boy, and Terrence Bonuku, a black lad from Zimbabwe," Mr. Epping said.

I reminded myself: Alfred-the-Athlete and Terrence-the-Teacher. "Yeah," I said. "How'd you know that?"

"The three are inseparable," Mr. Epping said. "Each is very bright. Beyond that, they are about as dissimilar as three lads can be. Their academic interests, physical traits, social rankings, but already they've bonded as closely as any three scholars I've ever had the pleasure to supervise. Should you become a fourth with them, I must warn you, they love mischief, especially your roommate, Mr. Tootlington. He may not appear as such, but I suspect he's their ringleader."

I laughed, remembering Tootles' odd sense of humor and the way the other two boys followed his lead. "That wouldn't surprise me a bit," I said.

"In addition to myself, there are other people who will be at your service," Mr. Epping said. "There is the house matron, Mrs. Etherington. She oversees a staff that clean and maintain Weatherby's rooms and public areas."

"I'll have a maid?" I asked.

"Not to yourself, of course," Mr. Epping said. "You will be expected to change your bed linens, send soiled clothes to the school laundry, polish your shoes and, in general, keep your area tidy. Other than that, they will Hoover the floors, clean the windows and perform other housekeeping duties as needed."

I nodded. "So when do I start classes?"

"We will arrange your schedule now," Mr. Epping said. "Follow me into my office."

We walked toward the front of the house and into a small room that looked out onto High Street. Mr. Epping settled himself behind a tall, roll-top desk. It was stacked with books and papers. He pointed to a nearby chair. I brought it close to the desk and sat down.

"Now, then," he said, taking a form from a drawer and a pen from his vest pocket. "Compulsory in the Shell year are English, geography and history." He entered the building name, classroom number and meeting time on the form. "Also, you will study a science and an art." He wrote "Comparative Anatomy" and "Early Dutch Masters" on the sheet. I guessed with that, he was done. Five classes seemed like plenty to me. Then he said, "You will also study information technology, mathematics, a language— French, Spanish, German or Russian—philosophy, and religious studies."

I stared at him in disbelief. He looked up and saw my bewildered expression. He smiled. "Well, not every day," he said. "Some courses will be studied in the spring and summer terms." Again he set his pen in motion and finished the sheet. "For your first day, I will escort you to the various buildings and classrooms. At each, I will introduce you to your teachers. Tomorrow you will be on your own."

I looked at the completed sheet and gaped at the enormous workload. I had a sudden urge to cry Uncle. Before I could, Mr. Epping withdrew his silver pocket watch and said, "Right. It's time for lunch. Let's go to the CDH, that's the Central Dining Hall. The boys humorously refer to it as the 'Trough.' I'm sure we'll meet Mr. Tootlington and the rest of your house members there."

The thought of food made me feel better. It was nice to know that I'd be given time to eat. "So, everyone has their meals together?" I asked.

"Like a family, which we are," Mr. Epping said. "Each house has about seventy lads, around fifteen in each of the five class years, Shell to Upper Sixth. We sit at the same three tables every day, just as we have for ages."

As he said this, a small black truck pulled up to the curb. "Sterns & Andrews" was painted in gold letters on the side. Out hopped the driver wearing a black cap and uniform. Another man in the same outfit jumped from the passenger's seat and met the driver at the back of the truck. They threw open the lift gate and unloaded an enormous trunk. "Where to, sir?" the first man said cheerily to Mr. Epping.

"All the way to the top floor, I'm afraid," he said. "Turn left and it's the last room on the right."

The two men moved past us and lugged the trunk up the wide staircase.

Mr. Epping looked at me and said, "Grab your duffel bag and we'll have a peek at your room, but we'll have to hurry. There'll be no time to sort your things and put them away. I'm sure Mr. Tootlington will help you with that later on."

We got to the room just as the two men were setting the trunk in the middle of the floor. I looked around and saw only one narrow bed, which had to be Tootles'.

"There you are, sir," the driver said. "The gents at the shop said to wish you all the best. If you need anything, don't hesitate to call."

I thanked them and they left.

"Right," Mr. Epping said. "Let's be off to lunch."

We crossed the High Street and hurried along the flagstone path to the dining hall where I had met Tootles, Terrence and

Alfred the week before.

I wondered how they'd react, now that I was not just a visitor but a real classmate. And Tootles, how was he going to take it, having to share his room?

Chapter Fifteen

⌒

The dining hall was full of boys, some standing and some already seated at their places. Mr. Epping led the way through the crowd, past guys laughing and talking loudly over the din. We neared the table where I had sat with Tootles, Alfred and Terrence the week before. And there they were.

Alfred-the-Athlete was looking our way. He nudged Tootles on his left and Terrence-The-Teacher who was sitting across the table from them. They looked up and all three waved for me to join them.

Mr. Epping left me and took his seat at the other end of the table.

"You made it in," Alfred-the-Athlete said.

I smiled as I looked from one to the next. All three really seemed glad to see me.

"And you're wearing our tie," Tootles said. "This means you're in Weatherby House."

"Yeah, and guess who's your roommate," I said. "I hope you don't mind."

"Are you joking?" Tootles said. "I was getting so bored with these two ignoramuses, they're the only other Shells on our floor. Their room is right across the hall from ours."

I noticed that he said "ours" and not "mine." He was already considering me an equal partner in the room. It was a small but telling point of acceptance.

"This is magnificent," Terrence-the-Teacher said, again

108

impressing me with his perfect English diction. "Now someone besides Alfred and me can help rein in our resident court jester." Then he added, looking serious, "You know, Michael, this will be no small feat, keeping Tootles out of trouble."

Just then, at the far end of the table Mr. Epping stood. "Gentlemen," he said. He waited a moment while the seventy boys at the three Weatherby tables quieted. "I would normally make this announcement at the house during morning callover, but today we have a special occasion."

Mr. Epping now had everyone's complete attention, including several tables nearby.

"I would like to introduce you to a new member of Weatherby House," he said. He nodded in my direction. "At the far end is Michael Hanlon." About seventy heads turned and stared at me. "Michael is not only new to Bulwick School, he has also just recently arrived from the United States. His parents were victims in the terrorist attack on the World Trade Center on September eleventh. He resides now in London under the care of his uncle. Last week, Michael sat for the same entrance exams as everyone else and achieved top marks in all. Still, life is bound to be different for him. I know each of you, as fellow Weatherbyans, will be very supportive as he learns his way around. Please give your new house member a warm welcome. Gentlemen, greet Michael Hanlon."

Everyone from the three tables stood and yelled, "Huzzah!" Even guys from other tables turned to see what the commotion was about. I looked around the room and saw boys, all dressed in the school uniform but wearing different colored ties, some green and silver, some red and gold, some blue and white. I figured each house must have its own colors. When everyone sat down, Mr. Epping said, "Michael, would you take a moment to say a few words?"

I looked around for what I hoped would be another Michael, someone holding some notes and ready to give a speech.

No such luck. I was the "Michael" he'd meant. I sat there not knowing what to do, but since everyone was staring at me, I stood up very slowly. That bought me about three seconds to think of something to say.

"Uh, well, uh, thank you very much," I said, smiling nervously.

Every eye and ear at the three Weatherby tables was fixed on me. I was about to make a first impression, probably a very lasting one, and my new schoolmates were about to cast a verdict.

I tried to clear my throat, which had suddenly become powder dry. "I wasn't really ready to give a speech," I said. "Everything has happened so fast, I mean, just two weeks ago I was in school back in New York, looking forward to playing football, meeting some new girls, seeing my old friends. Then…well, as Mr. Epping said, 9/11 happened and everything's changed. Now I'm here, and again, like Mr. Epping said, I'll need some help. I'm really glad to get into Bulwick School and I'll do the best I can to learn your ways." I looked along the tables to a sea of stares. I couldn't think of anything else, so I started to sit down.

Before I could, Tootles jumped from his seat and shook my hand. "Very well spoken, sir," he said loudly and with a theatrical bow. He turned to the assembled Weatherbyans. "How about another cheer for our new House member?"

The three tables huzzah-ed again. Tootles leaned in close and whispered, "You're not running for office, are you? Prime minister, king?"

Alfred-the-Athlete also stood at my side. "I'm impressed, too," he said. "That could not have been easy. I can't believe Mr. Epping introduced you so candidly. Was there anything he left out? Pimple on your bum?"

Terrence-the-Teacher, standing next to Alfred, said, "And to have you do it in front of the whole school? No other Fourth Former could have done it. I doubt a Sixth Former could."

"Well, I guess there's no sense beating around the bush," I said, as we all sat down. "Everyone might as well know why I'm coming in after the term has started."

Soon it was our turn to go to the food line. Everyone at our table got up and walked to the head of the cafeteria. I went along with the others and took my place at the back of the line.

As we waited, Alfred-the-Athlete asked, "When you said football, did you mean our football or American football?"

"American, I'm afraid," I said. "I still haven't gotten used to calling soccer, football."

"I was hoping that's what you meant," Alfred said. "I've seen some of your professional teams on television, and it looks a lot like our rugby. Can you fling a ball like American footballers do?"

"Sort of, I guess," I said. "Actually, that was my position. It's called quarterback. That's the player who does most of the passing. I can't throw it as far as the guys you saw on TV, but yeah, I know how to do that."

"Well, I'm planning on being the scrum half for our house team," Alfred said, "but I think we could use a bloke who can throw the ball like that. This afternoon, we're having our Shell team tryouts. We play seven-a-side rugby, and each house only has fifteen boys to choose from. I'm hoping you'd be willing to join us."

"Yeah, I'd like to," I said doubtfully. "But after lunch Mr. Epping is taking me around to my classes. Then I've got to get my stuff put away back at the house. Do you think I'd have time?"

"Sure," Alfred said eagerly. "We'll help you with your clothes, and the practice won't start until five. It'll work out perfectly."

"Okay, I'm game," I said. I picked up a tray and started along the cafeteria line. As I moved toward the front I realized I didn't have any money. I looked ahead to where a cashier might be, but didn't see one. "Where do we pay?" I asked Tootles.

"Here at the Trough?" Tootles laughed. "Believe me, it's paid for. You know that 25,000 quid? Meals, such as they are, are included. It's part of the character-building process, something we can look back on in forty years and laugh about."

"You're kidding," I said, and when I saw he wasn't, I filled my plate with three huge pork chops, a load of mashed potatoes and a major helping of some kind of pasta. I put two cups of strawberries and thick cream in a dish and stuffed an apple and an orange in my jacket pockets. I hurried to catch up with Tootles and followed him back to our table.

Tootles eyed my overloaded tray and deadpanned, "You're aware they'll feed us again tonight, right?"

I glanced down. "Uh, yeah, sure," I said. "It's just that I haven't had anything but ham sandwiches and potato chips since I landed in England. Everything looked so good. Think I overdid it?"

"Oh, no," Tootles said smiling. "But, believe me, you'll get over it." We made our way to the table. Ahead of us, Terrence and Alfred were already emptying their trays. Tootles and I set ours across from them and sat down.

"Did Mr. Epping prepare your class schedule?" Terrence asked.

"Yeah, it's right here," I said, pulling the sheet from my jacket pocket. I unfolded it and set it on the table. All three boys fished around in their book bags and spread their schedules next to mine. As they did, I dug into my first pork chop.

Alfred studied the four sheets. "Right," he said. "Your first two classes, English and French, are the same as mine. So, after breakfast we'll go to those together. Then we all have lunch here. After that, Tootles, I think you and Michael are in the next two classes together. Yes, see? Maths and science," he said pointing.

"So far, so good," Tootles said. "And look. After that, you

and Terrence are in theater together."

Terrence said, "And then we're all in the same religious studies class. That's the last one of the day. Between the three of us, we can take you through your whole schedule. You won't need Mr. Epping to show you around after all."

"Great," I said, "but do you think he'll mind?"

"Why would he?" Alfred said. "Besides, it'll be faster. After the last class, we could all run back to the house, put your stuff away and go to rugby."

"You're all trying out for the rugby team?" I asked. I didn't mean to stare at Tootles when I said it, but from what I'd seen of the game, I didn't think he'd last two minutes.

Tootles looked at each of us in turn, and then chimed in, "Yes, I know. You're all worried I'll beat you out for your favorite position. But fear not. If you try very hard, you'll be selected to the squad. Besides, I'll probably soon be moved up to the Bulwick Firsts."

Alfred looked at me and rolled his eyes. I smiled, not really sure what Bulwick Firsts meant, but it sounded like Tootles was putting us on.

"I'll just be playing to keep fit," Terrence said, looking my way. "My game is cricket, but that's not played until next summer."

Alfred-the-athlete said, "You understand, Michael, what we're talking about here is the Weatherby House Shell team, the Yearlings, the very bottom rung. Only Lower Fourth Formers from our house will be there. Each of the other houses will be using different fields for their own tryouts. Next week, our seven-man team will start playing the other houses. Actually, I'm hoping to move up to the all-school traveling team. Mr. Walker, Bulwick's head coach, will select the best players from all the houses and all the class years and put them on the school team, the Bulwick Firsts. We then have matches with Eton, Harrow, schools like that.

And Michael, if you can throw a rugby ball half as well as I think you can, you could make it, too."

I nodded, sort of understanding. I looked around and saw that most of the boys were moving toward the lunchroom door. I said, "When does our next class start?"

Alfred looked at his watch. "Half twelve," he said, getting up.

I did the math, but it made no sense. "Half twelve, –six?" I asked.

"No," he said with a laugh. "Half past twelve, twelve-thirty."

"And people think I talk funny," I said.

"You'll catch on," Terrence said. "I'll see you in theatre."

Mr. Epping came to take me to my classes.

Tootles bustled up to him and said, trying to sound like some movie star tough guy, "Move along, pal. We'll take the package from here."

Mr. Epping looked surprised at first, then smiled and turned away, shaking his head.

"The package?" Alfred asked.

"Heard it somewhere, Cagney movie," Tootles said. "Anyway, you've got to be firm with the hirelings or they'll start thinking they're in charge."

"Last time I checked the book," Terrence said, "I believe Mr. Epping is in charge, at least of us."

"Nonsense," Tootles said. "The book is just for show, impresses the parents. It confuses them into thinking the staff has a handle on things. We simply mustn't let them take it seriously."

Terrence and Alfred just looked at each other, rolled their eyes, and then picked up their bags.

We all moved to the door. Tootles and I waved to them as

they headed away.

For the next three hours I followed my new friends from one class to the next. I got books, took notes, and gathered assignments at each stop. I've never felt so lost in my life with all the different classes all over the place. Still, I never felt so welcome either. One or another of my new friends was with me every step of the way. Even so, it was almost too much.

Here's what I mean: I was in algebra, sitting next to Tootles, when the teacher, or "beak," as Tootles told me they prefer being called, anyway, as the beak chalked a math problem on the blackboard, he said, "X plus Y equals Zed." I whispered to Tootles, "What in the world is Zed? Some sort of constant? I've never heard of Zed before."

"No, you American twit," he whispered back. "Zed is the last letter of the alphabet, you know, X, Y, Zed."

"Oh, 'Z,'" I said, feeling better. "Man," I whispered, "even the letters don't have the same names around here."

Tootles just shook his head and smiled.

If he hadn't been right there to tell me what Zed was, I think I'd have picked up my pencils and packed it in. I sat back and breathed a sigh of relief. Still, it made me wonder what weird thing would happen next. It wasn't long before I found out.

Chapter Sixteen

We finished religious studies, or RS as Tootles called it, our last class of the day, and then ran back to the house. Tootles and I charged up the three flights of stairs to our room. Someone had brought in a second bed and set it across from Tootles' bed. It had the fluffiest comforter, thickest mattress and softest pillow I'd ever seen. This was a major step up from Uncle Sean's flimsy army cot, smelly horse blanket and scratchy sheets. Alfred and Terrence came in and helped me stow my stuff.

When we had most of it done, Terrence said, "Alfred and I are going to collect our rugby gear and head to the changer. We'll meet you there."

"What's a 'changer'?" I asked.

"It's where you change your clothes for outdoor sports," Tootles said. "We shower there after playing and leave the dirty stuff for the staff to clean. If you hadn't noticed, your name is on every stitch of clothing you wear. It's so they can bring it back to your room all clean, pressed and sweet smelling."

"So the changer is like a locker room?" I said.

Tootles nodded as he looked out the front window. "We'd better hurry. Several of our lads are already halfway to the pitch. Grab your kit and let's go."

I threw my rugby shoes, pants and striped shirt into a gym bag and followed Tootles into the hall. We met Alfred and Terrence and hurried down to a small room on the first floor. We changed into our rugby gear, crossed the High Street and trotted along the path to the playing fields.

The Bulwick School athletic grounds are a pretty impressive sight. A single rugby pitch is about the size of a football field, and Bulwick School has at least a dozen of them on a huge open area. The turf is like walking on an enormous golf fairway. And these are just the rugby practice grounds. In the distance I saw several cricket ovals, tennis courts and soccer fields. Beyond that was an entire golf course.

Our practice field was the farthest away, so as we passed the other teams, I saw that each squad wore shirts with their own house colors—stripes going vertically, horizontally, checkerboard even. It reminded me of pictures in English history books where knights in shining armor competed in tournaments. They'd be riding horses and wearing magnificent coats-of-arms. There would be jousting and archery. Fancy banners representing the various fiefdoms added to the pageantry. *Man,* I thought, *this is way cooler than our high school, college or even pro football. The American way is okay with its mascots, cheerleaders and marching bands, but this was on a whole other level.*

Finally, I saw a bunch of boys wearing the same red-and-black-striped jerseys as ours. Inside their circle was an older guy in classroom clothes, silk hat and all.

Alfred nudged me as we approached. He whispered, almost in reverence, "That's our coach, Oliver Hempstead. He's an Upper Sixth Former and scrum half for the Bulwick Firsts."

We were almost there when I could see Oliver turn our way. He was glowering at us as if we were enemy spies. I had seen that look on coaches' faces before, and it was never a good sign. Finally, he said, "Well, my fine fellows, it's nice of you to visit. By any chance, are you here for our house rugby tryouts?"

I looked over at Alfred. He nodded. "Yes, sir," he said, answering for all of us.

Oliver glanced at his watch. "Well, then," he said, "in that case, I must inform you that you are ten minutes late. If any of you has any intention of actually making the squad, you had better get up from your little afternoon naps and be on time with the rest of us."

"All my fault," Tootles said, stepping forward and looking contrite. "I was having a minor cardiac event, atrial fibrillation, I believe is the term. No, no, don't be alarmed. It probably would not have been fatal. But there I was, thrashing about on the pathway, when these three chaps rushed to my rescue. Fortunately for me, they recognized the severity of my state and commenced appropriate cardio-pulmonary resuscitation procedures. Regrettably, it took several minutes before I came to and, recognizing how long I had detained them, I begged them to attend me no further. I feared it would delay them from this, their crucial rugby tryout session. I beseeched them to hurry along to join their mates. But they, heroic lads that they are, simply ignored my pleas and proceeded to save my wretched life." Tootles then lowered his head, brushed a sniffle from his cheek, and added, "I promise, sir, it shall never happen again—only over my dead body."

"Right," Oliver said, holding back a laugh, but an upward curl of his lips gave him away. "Okay, all four of you, once around the pitch, full speed. Then you may join us, that is, if your little hearts can stand it."

We did the lap. Alfred, Terrence and I held back and ran along with Tootles so he wouldn't look quite so slow to our coach.

When we got back, Oliver Hempstead was sorting everyone by position. He looked at me. "You're the new American chap, right?" he said.

"Yes, sir," I answered.

"Ever play rugby before?"

"No, sir," I said.

"And what makes you think you can play it now?"

Rather bluntly put, I thought, but I was getting used to people speaking their minds around here. "Well, I'm a pretty fast runner and I've got a good arm," I said.

"A good arm?" Oliver blustered. "This is rugby. Cricket is next summer. We don't have a lot of use for 'a good arm'."

"Yes, sir," I said, wishing I'd kept my mouth shut.

Alfred spoke up, "Excuse me, sir," he said. "Maybe not the way you're used to playing it, but I asked Michael to come for a reason. I've watched American football on the BBC, and it seems the way they can throw a ball halfway across the pitch might come in handy in one of our matches. I'd like to see if our new member can do that."

Oliver studied me and said, "Is that right?"

"Uh, yes sir," I said. "I went to a game last week, and I think I can throw it as far as some of the players I saw."

"Right," Oliver said. He tossed me the fat white ball. "Give it a fling."

I caught it and juggled it back and forth between my hands. It was bigger around than an American football, but not as hard. I squeezed it, trying to get a feel for how well I might be able to throw the thing. I guessed I could do it.

I said to Alfred, "Go out a ways and cut across the field." I pointed where to run. He went about thirty yards downfield, broke to his left, and I let fly. The spiral caught him in stride and settled softly into his awaiting hands.

Alfred trotted back, winked at me approvingly and handed the ball to Coach Oliver.

Oliver Hempstead just stood, staring at me with his mouth open.

"Right," he said finally. "Michael, that's your name?"

"Yes, sir," I said.

"Right," he said again. "Go over there with the backs and listen to what they tell you. What you and Alfred did is all well and good, but there's a lot more to rugby than throwing the ball."

Actually, there wasn't a lot more to it, if you don't count butting heads with great big people or running for your life and then tossing the ball to the next guy, which I've always thought was more of a survival instinct than a taught skill. Besides, that was something I had learned back home playing football tag at recess.

By the end of the hour, my uniform was all grass stains and mud. I told Tootles that Weatherby House should change its colors to green and brown, perfect camouflage. The other team would never find us. Tootles said, "Great idea, but it'll never fly. I can already hear every Weatherby old boy rolling over in his red-and-black-lined coffin."

Anyway, the practice went pretty well. Toward the end, Oliver split us into two teams and we scrimmaged seven-a-side.

On about the fourth play, the ball came out of the scrum to Alfred. He tossed it to me, and as he did, he nodded that he was going to the opposite side of the field. I guessed at what he meant and continued to run in the direction of the play. As I neared the sideline, just before going out of bounds, I stopped, turned, and fired a bullet, quarterback-style, back across the field. There was Alfred, all by himself. The ball dropped into his hands and he strolled into the end zone for a "try," as they call a touchdown.

Everyone, even Oliver Hempstead, stood gaping, first at Alfred, who was still standing under the uprights, one foot on the ball and bowing to thousands of pretend fans, cheering wildly in a pretend packed stadium. Then the boys slowly turned their eyes in my direction.

"Did we just see what we just saw?" Tootles asked.

"He was wide open," I said with a shrug. "I could hardly miss him. Nice catch, though."

"Nice catch, my left foot," Tootles, said. "The throw was bloody brilliant." He turned to Oliver. "Are you sure that's permitted?"

Oliver shrugged, still gaping as us. "I can't think of any rule against it," he said.

Finally, after another ten minutes with Alfred and me hooking up for a few more long laterals, Oliver blew his whistle. He called everyone together. "Very well, gentlemen," he said enthusiastically. "I believe we have the basis for a first-rate, Shell rugby squad. If you continue your work ethic and arrive on time for practice," at that, he glared at each of the four of us, "we will do Weatherby House proud by season's end. Now run along and clean up for supper."

As we walked off the field, I heard someone shout, "Alfred, Michael." I turned. It was Oliver Hempstead. "If I may have a word before you leave."

Alfred and I looked at each other and then walked back to the coach.

"Boys," he said, "I see some raw talent in each of you. You're both too young for the Weatherby House squad, but with hard work, you may make the Bulwick School Yearlings, the Shell traveling squad, for visits to neighboring schools."

"All due respects, sir," Alfred said, "that might be good enough for some, but Michael and I have our sights set on playing alongside you for the Bulwick Firsts. Right, Michael?"

I had no idea what he was talking about, but I sensed a swagger in his voice. I stuck out my chin and said, "That's right, sir."

The Sixth Former smiled and waved us away. As he turned I heard him mutter, "Shells."

Chapter Seventeen

O liver talked to us for only a few seconds, but it was enough to convince me that I could win a place on the Weatherby House Shell team. Alfred's notion of making the varsity, the Bulwick School Firsts, was his, not mine. I'd seen some pretty big guys that day at the Trough, and I was sure I didn't want to butt heads with any of them, teammates or not.

We started along the path and I saw Terrence and Tootles walking just ahead of us. Alf called out to them and we trotted to catch up.

As we fell into step, Tootles said, "What was that all about? Oliver wasn't still calling you out for being late, was he?"

"No," I said. "He just told us to work hard and we might make the school Yearling team."

Alfred quickly added, "And I told him to watch his back because one of us was going to bump him off the Bulwick Firsts."

I nudged him and said, "You did not."

"Well, not exactly," Alfred admitted. "But I bet we could give some of them a good run for their money."

Terrence said to Alfred, "We mustn't forget to stop at the library and sign out that botany book."

"Oh, right," Alf said. He turned and said, "Michael, Tootles, we'll see you back at the house."

At that, Terrence and Alfred moved off on a different path.

Tootles and I continued toward Weatherby House. As we walked, six guys, each wearing purple rugby shirts with wide, horizontal white bars, came along from behind. By their dirty uniforms, I guessed they had been doing the same thing we had for the past hour. They were laughing and talking loudly.

The biggest one, a dark-haired guy in the center of the pack, pushed his way up to us. As he walked past Tootles he stuck his elbow out, jamming it into Tootles' ribs. It was a little too hard to be a friendly bump. I looked into his eyes and saw the same hostile glare I'd seen on Joey Cardle's face the year before.

Tootles looked surprised but said nothing.

"So," the kid barked, snorting to the others, "this is what Weatherby House is planning its rugby team around, a Yank footballer and Porky Pig. How pathetic."

A few of them laughed, but the others just stared.

"Hey, Tubby," the boy said, shoving Tootles in the chest. "You don't seriously think you can play this game, do you? Rugby isn't no sport for little fatsos."

At that, he snorted and pushed Tootles hard with both hands. Tootles fell backwards, landing square on his rear. Tootles adjusted his specs, got to his feet, and looked the kid right in the eye. He smiled and said softly, "Isn't any."

"What did you say?" the big kid shouted.

"Properly spoken," Tootles said calmly, "you should have said, 'Rugby isn't any sport for little fatsos.'" He winked at the kid, nodded to me and started to walk away.

The boy gazed dumbly at Tootles. His purple-and-white-shirted friends also stood speechless, like they were trying to figure out how the chubby little Weatherby Shell had put a lid on their loudmouthed teammate. Finally, a tall, skinny guy laughed and said, "I believe the little twerp has you there, Billy."

"Yeah, Monmouth, let's go," another said. "We'll be late for supper."

So, that was the jerk's name, Billy Monmouth. My memory

trick put "Billy" with "Bully" and "Monmouth" with "Monster-mouth." Yeah, I thought, Bully Monstermouth, I won't forget that.

Billy Monmouth jumped in front of us again and stuck his nose not more than an inch from Tootles' face. "You're telling me how to talk? I'll show you, you..." he stammered violently. "I'll see you on the pitch, you little pig, and when I do, you'd better be ready to squeal real loud or I'll drive you so far into the ground it'll take a steam shovel to dig you out."

I stood with Tootles, not knowing what to do. I looked from Billy to the other guys. They looked uncomfortable, embarrassed even.

Billy turned from us and muttered something to his friends as they walked to their dorm. The sign on its front lawn read, Cromwell House.

Tootles and I stood, watching them go inside. I turned to him and saw that his eyes were wet.

"Come on," I said, "let's go. He's a loser."

"Yes," Tootles said softly. "I know exactly what he is, and he's living proof of what my dad says, 'Force is the weapon of the weak.'"

"He didn't look all that weak to me," I said.

"He is for a fact," Tootles said. "They're all alike, bullies. They're weak and they know it, so they act tough. It's a smoke screen. In a tight spot, he'd be the first one to cave."

"Well, I feel bad anyway," I said. "I should have done something. It happened so fast, I couldn't think of anything. Besides, you got him pretty good all by yourself. That was beautiful. Even his own buddies laughed at him for it."

As we walked, I remembered how Andy Lang had turned tail and run during my clash with Joey Cardle. I was glad I had stuck with Tootles and been there when it was over. Still, I should have done something, said something at least.

Tootles said, "That's all right. I used to get this sort of thing at my old school. I thought, now that I'm at Bulwick, the boys here would be smarter, more mature."

"Some people never grow up," I said. "You know what, Tootles? You really impressed me, staying calm like you did."

"I've had some practice," he said. Then he looked at me, smiled and said, ". . . as you did."

"Pardon?" I said. "As I did what?" I had no idea what he meant.

"No," Tootles said. "You should have said, 'staying calm *as* you did.' Not '*like* you did.' "

I waved my fist in front of him and laughed. "It's a good thing we're buddies," I said, "or I'd pop you one. I'm bigger than you are, you know."

Tootles just smiled. Still, I knew how he felt and what it was like to be a bully's target. I vowed I would make it up to him. Somehow, some way my chance would come.

My first day at Bulwick School ended with me sliding into my soft bed. As I turned off the light I was suddenly struck with a horrible thought, *What if I have a screamer?* I looked over to Tootles, thinking maybe I should warn him.

"Tootles," I said.

"What, Michael?"

"I've got this little problem," I said.

"I hesitate to ask," he said, "but I will."

"All right," I said. "Ever since 9/11, I get these horrible dreams. It's not like every night or anything, but when I get one, I can wake up a whole town."

"You don't need to be hugged and tucked in, do you?" he said.

I laughed, remembering that's exactly how Uncle Sean got me back into bed. "I hope not," I said.

"Fair warning," he said. "Maybe I'd better tuck you in."

"Thanks," I said, "I hope you won't need to." I pulled the covers over my head.

I didn't have a dream that night, but it didn't keep me from worrying about it.

A rule at Bulwick School is that guys can't leave the campus except for one weekend night every month. It was probably to keep kids from running home to mommy every time any little thing went wrong. For me, it wasn't a problem because, unlike the other boys, I had no real home to go to. I could go to Uncle's, but the idea of sleeping in the old army cot and eating ham sandwiches at Casey's were hardly incentives. On the other hand, going to Uncle's would give me a chance to see Felicity Brown, except I was sure Uncle would never approve of such a meeting. Maybe at term break when I had more than one day away from school, I'd have a better chance to see her.

The rule didn't keep parents from coming to the school. They could check on their kid anytime they wanted, and some did it regularly. Uncle Sean called on me only once, all duded up, but also a little sauced. We went with a few Shells and their families for dinner at The Old Thames Inn, a classy restaurant on the river. I could tell right away that Uncle Sean was uneasy with the other adults. Maybe he thought they looked down their noses at him for being a working-class Irishman. He could dress himself up like a lord, but he still talked with that coarse Belfast accent. To me, Uncle just sounded different, but I think it riled the guys' parents.

They didn't seem to mind how I talked. In fact, I think they asked me questions just to hear me say stuff. Maybe it reminded them of some relative who was living in the Colonies. And that was something else, one of them calling America the Colonies.

Well, that got Uncle going again. He went off telling them the US was ten times the country England was. He said the bloody English had no reason feeling superior to any country, let alone the United States of America.

Everyone sat, open-mouthed, staring at Uncle Sean. He just glared back. I wanted to excuse myself and duck out, but that was not an option. See, the Bulwick guys never said anything about the Colonies. In fact, there wasn't one guy who ever lorded anything over me, not even the Sixth Formers who would be the likely ones to snub a lowly Shell. And not the ones whose dads had titles, and there was a boatload of them, boys with names that started with Baron or Viscount. They all treated me like I was just one of the guys.

Still, the only titled boy that I knew really well was my friend Alf, Alfred-the-Athlete. I asked him once, "How did your dad get to be called a lord?"

He told me that it went back hundreds of years. In the 1600s, Queen Elizabeth gave some land to one of his ancestors. She told him to watch over it for her—collect taxes, keep the people in line, settle arguments. Alfred said having a title didn't mean much to him. Oh, it was nice for going to special events, horse races, Royal Ascot, places like that. His family always got to sit in the best seats, but he really didn't feel he deserved it just for being born to the right parents. Sometimes it was even a little embarrassing, people staring at him, and pointing and whispering.

I told him how weird all that royalty stuff seemed to me, coming from America where there are no dukes or anything. "Everyone has to make it on his own," I said. "Sure, some kids get a better start than others. That's partly why parents work so hard, to give their children a leg up. But there are all sorts of stories about rich kids who have lots going for them and still fall flat on their tails, getting into drugs and screwing up. And there are just as many stories about poor kids, kids without a prayer in the world who pull off miracles by busting their butts and making use of their talents. You hear of it a lot with athletes, but it happens everywhere—artists, musicians, doctors—you name it."

"That's true in England, too," Alf said. "I think anyone, privileged or poor, who sits around and does nothing, leads a pretty dreary life. The only thing worse than working hard and getting nothing to show for it is doing nothing and getting everything handed to you. I mean, where's the joy in that?"

I knew he meant it, too. All you'd have to do is watch Alf in a rugby game to know he wants to show his worth. He isn't going to be one to sit back and rest on his family's name, not when he can be his own shining star.

Anyway, it was mid-October when right out of the blue, Uncle Sean called Sir John. He said he wanted to pick me up for a night at his flat. That was Saturday afternoon. He came by taxi, dressed in his best duds, and went into Sir John's office to sign me out. He came over to Weatherby House, picked me up and we caught another cab. It was about five o'clock and dark by the time we got to his place. I asked him why, all of a sudden, he wanted to see me. But all he said was that he thought I should get away for a night. That was fine by me. I might even see Felicity Brown. But still, it seemed odd, so I pressed him.

He answered, "Casey was asking about you, that's all. And I thought you'd like to hear some singing."

He walked into his apartment ahead of me. I looked across the street hoping to catch a glimpse of Felicity, but she wasn't there. I thought for a second that I might knock on her door and ask her to come along, but I knew what Uncle would say.

"Okay," I said. "Any other reason?"

"No, Michael," he said. He sounded a little reluctant, like he was holding something back. "Maybe we should get out of these suits. Folks might think we're trying to show them up. I've still got the clothes you wore when we came from New York."

I changed into my jeans, a shirt and sweater. Uncle put on a faded tweed jacket and a pair of old slacks. We went straight to

Casey's.

As soon as we came in the door, Casey threw up his hands in mock amazement. He shouted with his phony Texas twang, "Way-ull, look who's he-yah. It's our long-lost, Ay-merican gentleman, sure it is."

Of course, everyone turned to see who Casey's target was. An old man called out, "Will you look who's gracing us with his presence? It's the Earl a' Sammich." That brought a bunch of laughs.

Uncle and I sat down and in about two minutes, Casey's son, Liam brought two plates of sandwiches, hay-um for me of course, and egg for Uncle. Along with it he added two bags of crisps, a lemon mineral and a pint of Guinness.

At about six o'clock the music started. A man with a push-button squeezebox, a concertina, came in and played some Irish jigs. Then a fiddler got there, and they did a few hornpipes. Soon, a guy with an Irish drum, a bodhran, showed up, and the three really got everyone jumping, dancing, and carrying on.

Uncle ordered a second pint for himself and another mineral for me. I watched and listened as everyone got louder and rowdier by the minute.

A man came in with a guitar and joined the others for several songs. He passed it over to Uncle Sean who did two numbers before handing it to me. Remembering Uncle's advice about knowing my audience, I decided on an American Civil War song. "Lorena" is a story about a Georgia private who goes off to war, leaving his girlfriend behind. It's a little-known fact that Confederate generals banned "Lorena" from being sung in their camps because their soldiers would get so homesick when they heard it, they would desert during the night and head home.

While I was singing it, I looked up and saw Pearse Devlin, Uncle Sean's friend from Belfast. He came in and stood near the door. Immediately, Casey sent Liam to him, carrying a glass of whiskey. Pearse sat down and eyed me closely while I finished my song. When I had, he came over to our table.

"Sean," he said pleasantly, "could I have a few minutes with Michael?"

Uncle said, "Aye, of course, Mr. Devlin." At that, out of the corner of my eye, I swear I saw Uncle flash a knowing look at the Belfast man. I wondered, *What was that all about?*

Chapter Eighteen

~~~~~~~

Pearse Devlin nodded to me and I followed him behind the bar. We moved past Casey and into the back room. Again, he took a seat behind the desk and pointed to a full-sized chair in front of him. Someone had put it where the short stool had once been so when I sat down, I was facing him eye to eye.

"How's it going at Bulwick?" he said, sounding as pleasant as his gruff voice would allow.

I couldn't tell if he was trying to be polite or if he really wanted to know. Maybe he was just breaking the ice. I took the safe route and answered, "It's going okay—doing all right in my classes, playing rugby, making some friends."

"Such as?" Pearse asked. He said it like that was the whole point of me being there.

His tone surprised me. "You mean, other guys?" I asked. Why would he want to know that? To him, they're just boys, privileged and well-heeled, but so what?

"Aye, who have you gotten to know?" he asked. He seemed really interested.

"Well, my three best friends are all first years. 'Shells' they call us," I said. "We live in the same place, Weatherby House. Two of them are just across the hall: a black kid from Zimbabwe, Terrence Bonuku, and a white guy, Alf Noyes. My best friend though is my roommate, Tootles."

"Tootles?" he asked, leaning forward. "Is that his first name or last name?"

"Well, it's his nickname," I said. "His real name is Walter

Tootlington."

"Tootlington, eh?" Pearse said, smiling slightly and raising an eyebrow. "What do you know about him?"

"Tootles? Well, he's short, pudgy and about the funniest kid I've ever met," I said. "He plays rugby for our house team. To look at him you'd think he wouldn't survive his first scrum, but he's tougher than he looks. Hangs in there like a real trooper, outworks everyone, even Alf Noyes, our best player."

"What about his family?" Pearse said. "Where's this Mister Tootlington from?" He was trying to sound nonchalant, but when he said Tootlington, there was a cold edge to his voice.

"Here. England," I said.

"Where in England?" Mr. Devlin pressed.

"I don't know, north somewhere, Yorkshire, maybe." I wondered why Pearse Devlin would want to know all this stuff about Tootles.

"Did this Tootles ever tell you what his father does?"

"For a living?" I asked.

Pearse nodded.

"No, not that I remember," I said.

"Did he ever mention that his dad was in the House of Lords?"

"Oh, no, not Tootles' dad," I said. "Alf's father might be. He's Lord Noyes, Earl of Kent or something. Alf's the one across the hall from me. Tootles is just a regular kid."

Mr. Devlin stared at me, and then said, "So, this Walter Tootlington didn't have a roommate until you got there, right?"

"That's right," I said.

"Don't first year boys usually have a roommate?"

I thought about all the other Weatherby Shells. "I suppose,"

I said. "Maybe the guy couldn't come, got sick or something."

"And second year boys, they have roommates, too, right?"

I'd never thought about it, but he was right. Every Remove I knew did have a roommate. Mr. Devlin had done some homework. "Yeah, I guess," I answered. "I'm not sure about the other houses, but it's probably the same for the whole school."

"So, wouldn't you think, if there was a single room to be had, it would go to a second year student? Or maybe the son of a lord, like, who'd you say, the Noyes boy?" Pearse asked.

"Yeah, I suppose," I said. "I don't know anything about that."

Pearse couldn't hold back a self-satisfied grin. I felt like I'd just hand-delivered secret information that made his whole day. His smirk was almost more than I could stand.

Suddenly, he changed the subject. "You know," he said, "you've got a real talent with that guitar."

"Uh, thanks," I said.

"And your uncle tells me that you're a good student. You like history?"

After all Mr. Devlin's questions about Tootles, I was a little leery about where this was heading. "Yeah, I like history," I said, "Especially if it has to do with places I know something about, you know, America, England or Ireland."

"So, with your knack for singing and interest in folk music, I would think you'd like songs about history, the places you know about," he said.

"Sure," I said. "Back home I was really into American Civil War songs. Their lyrics are usually just the tip of the iceberg. The stories behind the songs are even better."

"I'm sure they are," Mr. Devlin said, in a patronizing tone. "But how about Irish songs, the ones your uncle sings?"

"Yeah, I like them, too," I said. "It's a lot different here. Back home, most people, especially kids my age, don't take much interest in folk music, but people here really get into theirs."

Mr. Devlin's voice became so soft I could barely hear, but I swear he said, "You're soon going to find out."

"Pardon?" I said.

He ignored me, but went on in his normal tone, "You know, when you do your American songs, people really listen. That's a rare talent for someone your age—being able to hold a crowd. I wonder if you could do that with an Irish song. Your father, Brendan, had a knack for that, too. Did you know that?"

"Uncle Sean told me about it when we got here, but before that, no, I didn't," I said. "Dad always kept a guitar at home, but I never heard him play it. I thought he only kept it for Uncle Sean."

"Oh, Brendan played, all right," he said, leaning back in his chair. "And when he did, old men saluted and young men marched."

"Uncle Sean told me that, too," I said. I remembered Uncle telling me about the Irish guy who ran out into the street and shot the British soldier.

Pearse said, "I just wanted you to know what fire your father had in him when he was your age. I think he'd be proud if you carried on that tradition. Would you like that?"

"Well, I guess," I said. "Uncle Sean told me that Dad was a hero."

"Brendan Hanlon wasn't just a hero," Pearse said. "He was a legend." Mr. Devlin leaned forward in his chair. "Now listen. Two boys are coming to Casey's tonight. They'll be singing some songs. I'm going to ask them to do one in particular. I want you to pay close attention to it. If you can sing that song the way Brendan did, it would make your old man proud. Will you do that for me?"

I felt I owed him this much, him being my dad's old friend

134

and all. Besides, what harm could that do? I mean, it's just a song. "All right, Mr. Devlin, I'll try. What song is it?"

Pearse leaned back again and said, "You watch the crowd. You'll know. I'm glad we had this talk." At that, he tossed down the rest of his drink, stood and walked out of the room. As the door was swinging shut I saw him nod to Uncle Sean. Uncle nodded back. A second later, Mr. Devlin was gone.

I watched, trying to sort the whole thing out. It occurred to me that maybe I was being set up for something. But how, and for what? I finally shook it off, stood, and then walked toward Uncle Sean's table.

Just then two men carrying instrument cases came through the front door. When Uncle Sean saw them, he waved them to our table. They smiled and sat down. One pulled a guitar out of its case and the other a fiddle.

As I got to my chair, Uncle looked up and said, "Oh, there you are, Michael. What did Mr. Devlin want?"

"Not real sure," I said. "Just seeing how I was doing, I guess."

"Good, good," Uncle said. "He's a fine man, Mr. Devlin. It never hurts to know people in high places." At that he motioned for me to sit down. "Listen," he said, "I want you to meet these two lads, Dominic and Seamus Logan. Boys, meet my nephew, Michael Hanlon."

I guessed them to be somewhere in their thirties, not quite as old as Uncle. They spoke with the same accent as Uncle did, the same way Dad talked when he got upset, like when Mr. Cardle called our house that night. I wondered if these were "the boys" Pearse Devlin had told me about. I figured I'd find out soon enough, you know, by listening to their songs.

As they tuned up, Dominic played fiddle and Seamus, guitar, there were shouts from all around for them to do one song or another.

"The Rising of the Moon," called one man.

"Foggy Dew," hollered another.

Dominic nodded as he strummed softly. The place slowly quieted.

Seamus looked at his brother. I heard Dominic say, "Let's start light."

Seamus smiled and hit three quick chords. Off they sailed into a wild version of "Rothsea-o." They followed that with "A Jug of Punch," which had everyone laughing and singing at the tops of their lungs.

The brothers waited patiently and carefully re-tuned their instruments. As they did, their expressions changed from mirthful and merry to somber and serious. Casey's crowd quieted as Dominic drew his bow through a slow introduction. It was a hauntingly beautiful tune, one I'd never heard before. Seamus joined in, softly picking notes in a minor key. There was not another sound in the place. Even Casey stopped his constant task of drawing pints. In perfect harmony, Seamus and Dominic lifted their voices.

The song was more powerful than any I'd ever known. It told the story of a twelve-year-old boy who held an entire regiment of soldiers at bay. As he did, his father, his brothers, and a dozen friends escaped capture at a place called Tannahill Bridge.

The hero of the song, a boy named Connor Flanagan, stood his ground while gunshots flew all around him. He defended himself with only a pair of pistols. Just as the last of his comrades slipped behind him over the bridge to safety, Connor ran out of bullets. An enemy soldier charged the bridge and shot him through the heart.

The song ended with the lines:

When we fight for our homeland like Connor The Bold,
We'll crush our cruel tyrant–free us all from her hold.

Seamus and Dominic let their voices, and then their instruments' notes fade. The brothers faced the audience, their expressions blank.

I stared at the two musicians and was surprised by how quiet Casey's had become. There was no cheering, no clapping, nothing. I looked at Uncle Sean. Tears were flowing down his cheeks. I glanced around the room. There was not a dry eye in the place. Still, neither of the Logans moved.

I heard a man whisper behind me. His voice was choked with emotion. "Good on yeh, sons," he breathed.

One man near Casey's front door started a slow, rhythmic applause. Suddenly, everyone jumped from his chair. The place erupted with a clamor of shouting, foot stomping and cheering, the likes of which I had never seen before or since.

This had to be the song Pearse Devlin wanted me to learn. Still, I wasn't really sure what it was about. The words said only that some boy had given his life to save his friends. There were names and places I'd never heard before, but I wanted to learn the whole story. I had to put it to memory. I had to be able to sing it. It wasn't something I wanted to do. It was something I had to do.

I looked at Uncle Sean. He was blubbering like a baby. I was embarrassed, seeing him like that, but I had to know. "Sorry Uncle," I said, "but could you tell me the name of that song?"

"'Connor Flanagan's Stand,'" Uncle said, his voice cracking.

I turned to the stage and watched the Logan boys do a few more songs. Then Casey said, "Right, lads," and I knew it was closing time.

I moved over a couple of stools. Dominic and Seamus began packing their instruments. I said, "Excuse me?"

Dominic said, "Yes, Michael."

"I was wondering if you might have time to write the words

to that 'Connor Flanagan' song?" I asked. "I'd like to learn it."

"That I can," Dominic said. He turned to the bar where Casey was pulling a last call. "Casey, do you have a scrap of paper and a pencil I could borrow?"

Casey nodded and went to his back room. He came out with a napkin, took a pencil from his apron and gave both to Dominic.

The fiddler dried the table with his shirtsleeve. As he wrote he said, "You won't find this in any book."

"Really? Why not?" I asked

"Not sure," Dominic answered. "We heard it at a rally years ago, I was around twelve. Seamus and I were with our dad in a back room IRA meeting. It was at a small pub in Newry. My brother and I would tape songs, take them home and learn them. A bloke not much older than us sang it. Next day, Dad told us the guy's family was killed by the RUC. Dad said it was because of the song he'd sung."

At this, Seamus leaned in to listen.

"Naturally, Seamus and I replayed the tape," Dominic said. "We learned it as quick as we could. One night Dad heard us practicing it. He told us we'd best leave that one alone. He said if the RUC ever heard us singing it, there'd be hell to pay. Well, we still worked on it, such a good story and tune, it was, but we decided we'd better not play it. Not in public, at least."

Seamus spoke up, "It's only been recently, after the Good Friday Treaty, that we dared sing it at all. We're both rank cowards, truth be told."

"Somehow Mr. Devlin found out that we knew the song," Dominic said. "We saw him at a pub last week, and he asked if we'd come tonight and sing it. 'Course, we could hardly say no to such a fine man as Mr. Devlin."

"Any idea who wrote it?" I asked.

"Not a clue," Dominic said. He thought for a moment and then added, "But that's true of most Rebel songs. The blokes who write them have always been a bit jittery about taking credit. If word gets out, their days, songwriting and otherwise, would soon be over. The event happened during the Rising of 1798, so it was probably written right after that, couple hundred years ago. It might even have been one of the Flanagan boys who wrote it."

In minutes Dominic had scrawled the whole song on the napkin. He slid it over to his brother.

"Seamus," he said. "Be a good man and mark this with the chords."

"Right enough," Seamus said. He took the pencil and scribbled some symbols above the words. "Here's a bit of a quirky part," he said. He put three chords over one word in the chorus. "If you get that right, it makes a nice touch. The bloke we heard that night in Newry ran that lick like it was nothing. It took me a year to get it halfway decent." He returned the pencil to Casey then handed me the napkin. "There you go, Michael. Be careful with it. It's one loaded song."

"Thanks," I said, wondering exactly what that meant. Seamus and Dominic finished their pints, picked up their instruments, and walked into the dark London night.

Uncle and I followed a minute later. As we went back to Uncle's flat, I hummed the Connor Flanagan tune over and over so I wouldn't forget it.

When I got there, I pulled my dad's guitar out of its case. I spread the napkin on the kitchen table and began playing the chords. I sang the words softly to myself, memorizing the lyrics.

Seamus Logan's warning, "one loaded song," kept buzzing through my head. What did he mean? And there was the strange feeling that Pearse Devlin was trying to get me to do something. That bothered me, too. Was I being set up or just being paranoid?

Chapter Nineteen

S unday morning I got up before Uncle did. I went across the street and went to Felicity's door.

I knocked. She opened it a crack, looking surprised. Instead of asking me in, she stepped outside and we stood near the street. "Michael, I've been so worried about you," she said. "Where have you been? Did your uncle do something to you? Are you all right?"

"Yeah, sure, I'm fine," I said. "I got accepted into Bulwick School, so I haven't been able to come back until yesterday."

"Bulwick School?" she asked. She looked amazed. "That's one of the most expensive boys' schools in all of England."

"Yeah, I know," I said. "It's a long story, but how's your school going?"

"It's boring," she said. "Mostly bookkeeping, not at all what I want to study. I'd like to be a doctor. I'd be good at that. But it takes so long and it's so expensive. There's no way. With my father out of work and me mum sick, I'm just taking courses that will get me an office job. And the sooner the better. The McDonald's one isn't nearly enough." She stared at me again. "But how'd you get into Bulwick School? I know your uncle could never afford that. No one living around here would even think of it."

"No," I said with a shrug, "but when Mom and Dad died, our house got sold and the money got put into a fund. Then a bunch of American charities sent donations to kids like me for schooling. Uncle takes care of it all." I looked at her and smiled. "Listen, I saw a notice at school, there's a dance coming up next month. I was wondering if you'd like to come?"

"To a Bulwick School dance?" she asked eagerly. Then she shrugged. "I hear those things are pretty much closed, like just to rich girls at the boarding schools."

"I don't know," I said. "The flyer didn't say anything about who could come. I'll check on it when I get back. If it's okay, would you like to?"

"Aye, of course," she said. "But I won't get my hopes up," she said. "Look, I've got to get back. I'm making breakfast for me mum." Then she said, "Hold a sec." She pulled a pencil from her pocket and scribbled on a note pad. "Here's my number. Would you ring me when you find out?"

"You bet," I said. "I'll call you tomorrow."

She smiled at me and went inside. It was one of those sad smiles—like she wished things were different and she could come to the dance. Like she wished we could see each other as often as we wanted, but she knew it never would be.

I went back to Uncle's flat. He was in the kitchen frying some eggs.

"Been over seeing your English bird, have yeh?" he said with a scowl.

"Yeah," I said. "You don't approve?"

"No," he said. "You're just like Brendan. First pretty face you see, you forget everything you've ever been told about who you are. You shouldn't have gone."

At four on Sunday afternoon I packed my dad's guitar and took the bus back to school. I was still thinking about Felicity when I ran up the steps into Weatherby House.

As I passed the Fourth Formers' common room I saw Tootles, Alf and Terrence playing two-on-one ping-pong. Of course, it was Alfred-the-Athlete against the other two.

Alf slammed a kill shot past Tootles and looked up. "Welcome back, Michael," he said. "How was your weekend?"

"Odd," I said. "But it was okay. I met some people, learned a song. Say, did any of you see that flyer at the Trough about a dance; I think it's next month?"

"The one with Wycombe Abbey?" Alfred said.

"Yeah, I guess," I said. "Can you ask any girl to it, like maybe just someone you know?"

"I don't think so," Alf said. "These things are strictly between the schools. They gather their girls and bring them here for a dinner and dance. Next week we do the same and go there. The month after that we go to another girls' school and so on. It's supposed to make us meet the proper kind of girl." Alf set his paddle on the table and stared at me with a sly smile. "You've got a bird haven't you?"

"Yeah, well, it's someone I met who lives near my uncle," I said. "When I asked her to the dance, she said she didn't think it was allowed."

"I'm afraid she's right," Alf said. "Schools like ours try to keep its boys removed from what they consider 'unworthy' social relationships."

"Well I, for one, think Felicity's pretty worthy," I said. "Now I almost wish I hadn't asked her."

"Don't give up so fast," Tootles said. "There may be a way around it."

That sounded like wishful thinking. I watched Alf toying with Terrence and Tootles at ping-pong, thinking how I would have to call Felicity and break off our date. When you hear people say, "Be careful what you wish for," it's true. I wanted so bad to get into Bulwick, and now, because I'm here, I can't invite someone who's not on the school's "A" list. Right then I decided on making good another old saying: "Where there's a will, there's a way." Maybe Tootles was right, and I'd be able to keep our date.

Just then I saw Tootles eyeing my guitar case. He said, "Is that really a guitar in there, or are you smuggling in a side of beef?"

"It's a guitar," I said with little interest. I was still thinking about Felicity.

Tootles turned back to the ping-pong match. "I'm surprised you never mentioned it, that you play guitar," he said.

"Uh, yeah. Well, I haven't had much chance to play the thing since I got here," I said. "I was in a little group back home, not rock or anything, just folk." I watched the game for a minute then asked, "Need a fourth?"

Alfred answered, "Sure, jump in. These two losers need all the help they can get. Grab a paddle. I'll play all three of you."

"Wait a minute," Tootles said. "This isn't tug-of-war. More isn't better. How about this: We'll play partners up to ten and switch after each game. The guy with the most wins before tea is the champ."

"All right," Alf said. "Michael, come over to my side." He tossed the ball to Terrence to give him first serve. As I took my place beside him, he said, "You haven't forgotten about tomorrow's game with Cromwell House, have you?"

"Not for a second," I said. Terrence served the ball into my court. "Cromwell. They're the guys that got in Tootles' face that day after the first practice. Billy Monmouth was the main goon, right?"

"That's right," Tootles said, hitting my return shot. "And I want to be there when you cream him."

"You're not playing?" Alfred asked, slamming Tootles' soft volley.

"'Course I'm playing," Tootles said. "I'm just not going to

be the one doing the creaming. Who do I look like, The Hulk? Oh, no. I'll leave the rough stuff to you boys."

"What are teammates for?" Alf said.

"Quite," Tootles said. "All for one and one for all, that sort of rot."

"Absolutely," Terrence said seriously. "I still can't believe a fellow Bulwickian acted so rudely."

"Actually, I can," Alfred said. "I'm in some classes with him, and he can be a right ass when he has a mind to be. He does it when he wants to impress someone. By himself, Billy's not a bad bloke, but when he's with his mates, he's a different sort altogether."

"He must have a dominant belligerence chromosome somewhere in his double helix," Terrence said.

We played for another half hour and kept switching partners until it was clear that Alfred was the champ. We headed up to our rooms to change for dinner.

After we came back from the Trough, I pulled the guitar from under my bed. I opened the napkin and flattened it on my desk. Tootles was stretched out on his bed, reading his world history book.

I played the chords softly and hummed the tune, keeping the words to myself. I remembered how the Logan Boys had stunned Casey's crowd the night before. If I could learn this song, I might try it at an open mike somewhere. Maybe Pearse Devlin was right. Maybe I really could hold an audience. If my father could do it, why not me? The few times I'd sung at Casey's went pretty well. His regulars probably weren't the toughest critics in the world, but their applause was sincere enough. It still bugged me, though—why did Mr. Devlin want me to learn this particular song?

Tootles looked up from his book and said, "Bloody good tune. Is that the song you meant when you got back from your uncle's?"

"Yeah," I said. "I heard it at a pub last night."

"You ought to play it for the talent show," Tootles said.

"What talent show?"

"The one in Debate Room Saturday night," Tootles said. "Didn't you see the notice at the Trough? It's been on the activity board for a fortnight. The whole school will be there. It gives lads like you a chance to show your stuff."

"Are you serious?" I said. "I couldn't do that. I just heard the song last night. Besides, I bet there are some pretty talented guys around here. I can just see myself, stepping on stage with my little trail guitar right after some Sixth Former has belted out a Bach concerto on his grand piano. Oh, yeah, I'd knock 'em dead, all right."

"Just a thought," Tootles said.

"Well, it doesn't sound like a very sane one," I said.

"Don't sell yourself short," Tootles said softly.

"I'm not," I said. "I'm just being realistic. Look, hearing a song and playing it before a crowd are two way different things. Besides, if the show is this Saturday, I'm sure they've had tryouts by now."

"They haven't. Auditions are this Thursday," Tootles said. "That's part of the gimmick, spontaneity. How about this: Let's say you work on your song for a few days, get a feel for it, and then go to tryouts. You get there late, put your name at the bottom of the list, and sit back. You see how good the other blokes are, and if they're out of your league, you simply tell the beak in charge that you think you're coming down with a broken wrist. Tell him you're having a cardiac event. That always works for me. Then you leave without actually making a fool of yourself. No harm in that, right?"

"Well, maybe not," I said with a laugh. I thought back to

Casey's and pictured the Logan brothers. If I could do "Connor Flanagan" half as well as they had, I may not win, but I'd be able to walk off stage with my head high.

As Tootles went back to his book, I looked at the napkin. The more I thought about it, the more I wanted to give it a try.

Chapter Twenty

W ith classes over on Monday, I started thinking about the rugby match with Cromwell. Actually, I hadn't stopped thinking about it all day, but since Alfred, Terrence and Tootles never said anything, I didn't bring it up either. All the other games we'd played up until then were just that, games. I didn't know any of the guys on the other teams, so I was just out there getting a feel for my position and having fun.

This one would be different. For me, it was a grudge match. Tootles wasn't the only Weatherby player put off by the Cromwell captain. With all that had gone on last year with Joey Cardle, Billy-The-Bully Monster-Mouth had me a little spooked, too.

We had played four matches and won them all, so we had a little swagger going. On the other hand, we'd only beaten Leslie House by a couple of tries and The Heath by one. Cromwell, also unbeaten, had clobbered both houses. Billy Monmouth, good sport that he was, did all he could to run up the scores. So, even though our records were the same, we were the clear underdogs.

Lately, Billy had been strutting around, telling anyone who would listen that he, as Cromwell captain, something he mentioned in about every sentence he uttered, was planning to crush Weatherby House. He was personally going to drive the little pig, as he called Tootles, into the ground and embarrass us so badly in the first half that we'd toss in the towel and not come out for the second.

Tootles and I were in the changer getting our gear on when Terrence and Alf came in.

"Are you boys about ready?" Alfred asked.

"Nearly," I said, tying my shoe. "What do we know about the Cromwell team, other than they've got a first-class jerk for a captain?"

"Not much," Alfred said. "Oliver says he's seen them practice. They're big along the front line and fast on the wings, but they've got nobody who can throw like you do. Oliver thinks we can take them off their game with a few of your long laterals."

I looked at Tootles. He was slowly lacing his boots. He had barely said a word since we'd gotten back from our last class, not like him a bit. I guessed at the reason. "Don't worry, Tootles," I said. "We'll get him."

He held his laces and stared at me. "You know, that's the annoying thing," he said.

"What's that," Alfred asked, pulling the striped jersey over his head.

"I didn't do anything to get him started on me, and yet I'm the one who constantly thinks about what's going to happen the next time I see him, whether it's in class, at the Trough or on the rugby pitch. Playing a game like this should be fun, right? I mean, that's what it's all about: exercise, fresh air, camaraderie. A bunch of lads dress up in house colors and run around, get dirty, sweat. Win or lose, what more could a bloke want? Instead, all I've done since the day I met him is dread this one. All because he wants to show his mates what a tough fellow he is, and of course, I just wandered along at the wrong time and became his personal punching bag."

"We'll take care of him," Alf said. "When he tries something, I'll put an elbow down his throat."

"No," Tootles said. "Remember the other day when I told you about creaming him? I've been thinking about that. I don't want you to cream him. That won't settle anything. It'll just make it worse. Look, it's not like I want him to be my best friend. I just want him off my back."

"I've got an idea," I said.

"A brilliant one, I hope," Tootles said.

"Last year, a guy a lot like Billy wanted to show off to his pals," I said. "It was my first day at a new school, and this bozo, Joey, must have sensed that I was like a lost sheep in a forest. He followed me around in the halls, needling me every chance he got. Then, on my way home, he and his pals cut me out from the herd. He was about to beat the snot out of me when I threw one lucky punch and decked him, knocked him out cold. The thing is, for being in a fight, the school principal made me take a class that I thought was a waste of time. Maybe it wasn't. C'mon, let's get going. I want to talk to Oliver Hempstead before the game."

We finished dressing and met the rest of the Weatherby Shells in the yarder, a small meeting area just outside the changer. The rest of the team was already there, waiting for us. I looked for our coach, but he wasn't around.

So we headed out, crossed the High Street and hurried down the long path to the playing fields. When we got close I saw the purple-and-white-shirted Cromwellians warming up at the far end of the nearest pitch. Several older members from both houses had gathered on the sidelines to watch the battle of the two unbeaten teams. The game had an air of excitement, sort of like cross-town rivals back in the States.

Standing between the two squads and talking casually were Oliver Hempstead and another older guy wearing Cromwell's purple-and-white tie. I recognized him as their coach, who like Oliver, was a member of the Bulwick Firsts. I hurried ahead of my teammates and trotted toward them.

"Excuse me, Oliver," I said. "Something's come up. You got a second?"

"Sure, Michael, I'll be right with you." He turned back to the Cromwell guy and wished him luck. Then he faced me and asked, "Something wrong?"

"Well, sort of," I said. I told him about the run-in Tootles had had with the Cromwell captain. "I've got an idea how to help."

"Let's hear it," Oliver said.

A minute later, Oliver brought us together. We stood in a circle as he gave us last-minute instructions. Then the referee blew his whistle to have the two captains come to the center of the field for the coin toss.

The Cromwellians ended their pre-game talk with a shout. Then out strutted Billy Monmouth, swaggering toward the referee.

Moments later, we broke our huddle, but instead of Alfred Noyes, our regular captain, Oliver sent Tootles. Even from where I stood on the sideline, I could see Billy Monmouth's face color and his jaw drop. He read our message, and he read it loud and clear. If he so much as bumped Tootles, he would have a whole bunch of red-and-black shirted guys stomping his face for the rest of the afternoon. If he didn't know it before, he knew it now: He had chosen the wrong guy to mess with that fateful day in September. The chubby little nobody he had thought he could push around was none other than the Weatherby House team captain, and nobody knew the importance of being team captain better than Billy Monmouth.

Tootles trotted to the middle of the field, smiling and staring Billy square in the eye all the way. When they met, the referee asked Tootles to call the coin in the air. Tootles called heads. It landed heads, and Tootles chose to receive, getting first possession.

The referee said, "Gentlemen, shake hands, and may the best team win."

Tootles nodded to the ref and said, "Yes, sir, we shall." He then reached his hand to Billy who looked down and took Tootles' grasp feebly. Tootles squeezed back with every ounce of strength he had. He wanted to make sure Billy remembered the moment.

Tootles then turned and jogged back to our side, grinning

all the way.

If there ever was a game where its turning point came a minute before the coin toss, this was it. Tootles had put Cromwell's best player on his tail with a handshake. As we lined up for the kickoff, I looked across the way and saw in Billy's eyes the unmistakable look of defeat. He realized he wouldn't dare live up to his boast of driving Tootles into the ground as he'd promised his teammates, and practically the whole school, not without serious injury to himself. For him, the game was up. The other Cromwellians might not have known it, but they would soon discover that one very significant member of their seven-man squad would be unaccountably missing.

After that, it was just a matter of time. I threw a couple of long laterals to Alf, and he ran them in for tries. Terrence scored when he picked up a ball that Billy Monmouth had fumbled. Every time Billy came within two yards of Tootles, he backed off. The Cromwellians on the field and along the sidelines must have sensed it, because by halftime they were shaking their heads at their captain's pathetic performance.

We won by a nice margin, but the exact score didn't matter.

It was pure joy watching Tootles locking arms with his teammates and going at it in the scrums, grinning like a two-year-old on Christmas. He was finally rid of his bullying nemesis.

As for me, I had made up for my feeble response when Billy Monmouth had confronted Tootles on my first day at Bulwick School in September.

Chapter Twenty-One

After the game we hurried back to the house, changed out of our grass-stained uniforms, showered and got dressed for dinner. Tootles and I went across the hall, knocked on Terrence and Alfred's door, and we all headed to the Trough.

As we went inside, Tootles showed me the notice board and pointed to the talent show flyer.

"There, see?" he said. "Auditions are this Thursday at seven, right after dinner. Think you can be ready by then?"

"I don't know," I said doubtfully.

"Hey," Tootles said. "If I can captain a whole rugby game, you can sing one folksong. Look, here's what you do: Tonight, take your guitar downstairs to the music room. It's soundproof, so you can make all the mistakes you want and nobody will hear you. You can even tape yourself and listen to how you sound. My guess is, you're your own biggest critic."

I thought that over as we took our places with Terrence and Alfred at the table. I just might be able to pull it off. After all, it is just one song.

Alfred smiled at each of us and said, "You know, today's game was the most fun I've ever had in my life, at school, in sports, at home, ever. What we did to Mr. Monmouth without laying a hand on him was worth more than any cheap shot I could have given him. You know, before the game, I wanted to tell him that if he placed one finger on Tootles, he'd better plan on taking an early exit from the match and a hasty visit to the infirmary. I wouldn't have cared one whit if the ref had tossed me out of the game."

"Billy Monmouth wouldn't have been worth it," I said. "I started to tell you about this in the changer, the guy I ran into a year ago back home. He was one nasty dude. He picked a fight with me to show his pals how tough he was. The four of them had me cornered and Joey was about to put me away. He let down his guard for a split second and I threw a punch. For good or for bad, it landed. Turns out, I almost killed him. But the thing was: I could have gone to jail for it. I don't know if he learned anything, but I sure did. First, bullies like Billy Monmouth and Joey Cardle, my pal back home, are best avoided. Second, if you can't dodge 'em, report 'em. Tell your parents or a teacher. Then, if that doesn't work, you've got one other choice."

I waited a second, hoping one of them would bite.

Alfred did. "And what might that be?" he asked.

"You out-friend 'em," I said with a smile.

"Pardon me?" Terrence said.

"You get more friends than he's got," I said. "I don't mean you go out and buy them, you know, get 'em stuff. But you do things with people, all kinds of people. You walk around school with your head up, smile, look confident. You talk to kids in your lunch period, get into class projects, join clubs, stuff like that. Look, a bully pushes around kids who he thinks won't fight back. It shows he's got power over them. Ever see one pick a fight with the school's best heavyweight wrestler? Of course, not. Unless he's stupid, too. Most bullies are cowards. Oh, they may not look or sound like it, but deep down, they are. They think if they can rile someone who they think won't stand up for himself, it will impress his pals. Now, let's say, this kid sees you, and you're buddies with a bunch of guys. It makes him think twice about taking you on."

"I never thought of it like that," Alfred said, "but it makes sense—in a twisted sort of way."

"I'm not sure about that last part, Michael," Tootles said, "but you're right about the first two: steering clear of trouble and reporting a bloke when he gets in your face. Still, that only works if the person you tell, teacher or whatever, is willing to do something about it. Some people, even teachers, don't want to listen, especially if you whine. They think, 'Of course he's getting picked on. He's a crybaby.' So, they turn their backs on you, particularly if the bloke in question is popular, an athlete or something."

"You've been through this before?" Alfred asked.

"I have," Tootles said. "A couple of years ago there was this one kid, Harold Gross was his name. He teased me about my glasses, my size, my name. He made up all sorts of ignorant stuff. It got so bad none of my friends would sit with me at lunch or even talk to me. They were afraid Harold would turn on them, too."

"So, what did you do?" Alfred asked.

"I did what Michael said," Tootles answered. "I took it as long as I could and finally I told my teacher. Unfortunately, the teacher was also the school cricket coach. Harold Gross, as luck would have it, was his best batsman."

"No help there, right?" Terrence said.

"None," Tootles said. "But then I went to the headmaster. With him, I caught a break. He actually listened to me and took the time to see what was going on. Then he did something about it. He told Harold's parents that their son was a little terrorist. He threatened them that he would expel their kid if he didn't shape up. I was lucky with that, too. Some parents wouldn't see a time bomb ticking on their sweet little lad's nose, but Harold's parents listened. Anyway, Harold changed overnight. By the end of the school year, we even started to get along, sort of."

We had been sitting at the dinner table for a few minutes when our coach, Oliver Hempstead, stood and said, "Fellow Weatherbyans, please join me in giving our undefeated Shell rugby team a hearty cheer for its victory this afternoon. Gentlemen, hip,

hip…"

Every house member shouted, "Huzzah!"

"And now," continued Oliver, "let's hear it for the man who led his squad to victory. Three cheers for the captain, Walter Tootlington!"

Three huzzahs rang out with every Weatherbyan on his feet.

When the applause died down, I looked across several tables to where the Cromwellians sat. They all were looking our way. Had Billy Monmouth heard the cheer for Tootles? You bet he had.

After dinner, I went straight back to the house. I told Tootles, "I'm going to the music room."

"You're trying out for the show?" he asked.

I nodded.

"That's the spirit." he said. "You can do it."

I put a blank cassette in my pocket, picked up my guitar and headed down the stairs.

For the next hour I worked on the song. When I thought it was sounding pretty good, I put the cassette in and taped it. I punched 'play' and realized how lousy I sounded. I'd rushed some lines and muffed the triple chord change in the chorus. My voice was weak in places where I should have hammered points. *No way am I going on stage sounding like this,* I thought.

I tried it a few more times and then put the tape back in. It came out a lot better, still not great, but better. I decided I'd give it a good night's sleep and see how it sounded the next day.

I came back to my room as Tootles was closing his RS book. As he crawled into his bed, he said, "Thanks."

"For what?" I asked.

"For what you did at today's match," Tootles said. "Getting

Oliver to make me captain."

"Oh, that," I said. "I just told him that we should have our team leader handle the coin toss and, Tootles, that's you. Alfred can play circles around all of us, but you're the guy everyone looks up to. They see it when you take on the other team's biggest forwards and tackle their strongest runners."

"Well, if that's all that's holding us together, then we're in a lot more trouble than I thought," Tootles said with a laugh. He tossed his RS book onto the floor, rolled over and turned off his light.

The next day between classes, I saw Billy Monmouth walking toward me. I happened to be alone, but he was with some of his rugby teammates. This time, he wasn't in the center of the crowd but a little to the side and a step behind. Still, I expected him to make some sarcastic comment, either directly to me or, more likely, aside to his friends about me. But as I stared him in the eye, he lowered his head. I recognized one of the guys he was walking with, a forward on the Cromwell team, so I nodded to him.

The kid smiled and nodded back. That was it. Maybe it was my imagination, but I was pretty sure Billy Monmouth had dropped several rungs on Cromwell House's social ladder.

Thursday after dinner at the Trough, I used Tootles' idea and waited before going to the talent show tryouts. From my window, I could see other guys carrying instrument cases on their way there. It was supposed to go from seven to nine, so I hung around outside to make sure I'd be last. At about 7:15, I signed in. The beak in charge told me I could sit out front with the other guys and watch until he called me. *Perfect,* I thought. *Tootles, you're a genius.*

The place is known as the Debate Room, but it's actually an entire building, like an ancient Roman amphitheater with an impossibly high, beautifully arched, dark wood ceiling. It has

Gothic columns and ancient, stained glass windows. The stage is at one end and the seats form a half circle going straight up almost all the way around the podium. So, if you're the one on stage, you're a sitting duck for anyone with a ripe tomato and halfway decent aim.

The first time I saw the place was for the headmaster's weekly Monday morning announcements, which the whole school had to attend. I walked in with Tootles, took one step through the door and just stared. The place was awesome. We made our way up in the nosebleeds and sat down with the rest of the Shells. From there, when Sir John spoke, even without a microphone, I could hear every word he said.

Anyway, tonight, as I signed in on the tryout sheet, I checked the roster of about twenty other boys who'd gotten there before me. After each name was the guy's year, his house, and what he did. None of the acts sounded like showstoppers. One kid, an Ashfield Remove, was doing a speech from *Hamlet*. A Sixth Former from Leslie House was playing a bassoon solo. I mean, how hard could it be to beat them out?

I recognized only one name on the list. A kid from my own house, a Fifth Former, Cuthbert Glanville, had a magic act. You'd have to know this guy to see how his being here would boost my confidence. Cuthbert was shy, quiet, and almost invisible around the house. Maybe, that was his magic trick, making himself invisible. I knew for sure his routine would be lame.

I smugly carried my guitar up the aisle and sat down behind the others. The first few guys weren't bad, and I realized I'd have to do pretty well to make the cut. Then, if I did, it would only be two days before I'd be in front of the entire school. My mouth started getting a bit dry, and I wished I'd brought some bottled water.

As I watched one guy after another, I slowly realized how badly I had underestimated them, even the bassoon solo. I was glad when it was Cuthbert's turn, knowing how feeble his act would be. As he walked onstage, he was sweating like a pig, and I sort of felt sorry for him. He smiled nervously and started with a couple of dumb handkerchief tricks, which had everyone groaning.

Suddenly, Cuthbert's wand flew out of his hand. It circled crazily over his head, completely out of his control. Then, right out of thin air, a fuzzy yellow duck popped up from behind his head. It landed on his shoulder and stared at the audience, looking in one direction then the other without a sound. Cuthbert looked at it in amazement, like he had no idea how it got there. Then the goofy bird started gyrating crazily and sang, "We all live in a yellow submarine."

Mind you now, there were only about twenty people watching this, the beak and the guys trying out for the show, but I thought the place was going to explode from the laughter. For the next two minutes guys were falling out of their seats, holding their sides and gasping for air. By the time Cuthbert left the stage my ribs, my face, my whole body hurt.

I looked at my little guitar and knew I was in over my head. I had to get out of there, but before I could move the next guy started. I was so taken by his act that I forgot to look for the exit. Several more boys followed, and as the last one walked off stage, I heard someone call my name. It was the beak.

I was up. I walked unsteadily to center stage. I must have looked like an idiot as I stood there, fumbling to hook the guitar strap.

"Go ahead, Mr. Hanlon," the beak said. It was late and he sounded tired.

"Uh, yeah, right," I said. My voice echoed throughout the building.

Let me say this right now. If you have never tried out for a talent show, especially as a solo, you may not know this. I don't care how many times you've rehearsed your number or how simple a song it might be, if you're not one hundred percent ready, it's like a curtain drops over your head. You hold your instrument, it could be a tin whistle or kazoo, and it feels like an anchor. Your mouth goes absolutely powder dry and your heart slams into your throat. The room spins and you wonder whatever possessed you to do this.

This is called stage fright and I had it big time.

For what seemed like a whole minute my mind went totally blank. I couldn't even think how "Connor Flanagan" started. I had forgotten Tootles' plan, but his "cardiac event" idea would not have been far off.

"Mr. Hanlon?" the beak repeated.

With a stroke of luck, my left hand made a D-minor chord, and I strummed the strings a few times. Somehow, muscle memory maybe, my fingers moved to an A-minor, then an F, a C and finally another D-minor. I went through that sequence twice before the first word of the song popped from my mouth.

Actually, I don't even remember singing that first line, but I must have, or how else would I have gotten to the part where I played a G chord instead of a C and then skipped an entire verse of the lyrics? After that, the next thing I remember was that I had finished. I stood there shaking. There was an eerie silence, no applause, nothing.

I looked up. Except for the beak, no one was there. Then I realized: Of course not. I was the last one to try out. Just because I had watched everyone else's routine, there was no need for them to stick around to see mine. It was after nine, time for lights out.

"Very well, Mr. Hanlon," the beak said dryly. "I must say that was a most unusual selection, but I'm sure you have your reasons. Be that as it may, you may check the board at the dining hall tomorrow. The list of contestants will be posted before breakfast."

I nodded to him, glad that no one else had been there to witness my pitiful performance. I knew I wouldn't make the show, but at least, I'd learned my lesson. Never again would I step on stage without practicing my number a thousand times. I'd know it so cold I couldn't possibly make a mistake. If I sounded like a robot, it would still be better than stumbling around like I had today.

I packed my guitar into its raggedy case, escaped through the exit, and walked slowly back to Weatherby House. I trudged up the three flights of stairs and down the hall to my room. I turned the knob and eased myself in. A tiny night light aided me to the side of my bed. As quietly as I could, I slipped my guitar under my bed, stripped down to my skivvies and pulled the blankets over my head, hoping for a quick nod off to sleep. No luck. I stayed awake for hours.

Chapter Twenty-Two

Next morning, Tootles and I went to breakfast and met Alfred and Terrence outside the Trough. As we went in, we passed the message board. I let the others go ahead, hoping no one would see me looking at it.

No such luck. Alf turned to me. "Hey, Michael," he said. "You're unusually interested in the notices this morning. What's up?"

Tootles answered for me, "He tried out for the talent show last night, and the list is posted today. I think he's hoping not to find his name there. Right, Michael?"

I muttered, "It wouldn't be the end of the world." Then I looked at Tootles, "But what makes you think I don't want to make it?"

"Because of how, when you got back from the Debate Room, you came in so quietly I guessed you didn't want to talk about it," Tootles said. "Was it that bad?"

"Yeah, it was worse than bad," I said. "See, the thing is, the song itself is amazing—terrific tune, great story—everything. But I'm glad you weren't there to watch. I mucked it up royally. I'm sure I didn't make the cut."

Tootles moved to the far end of the notice board and pointed. "At the risk of disappointing you, I believe I've found your answer," he said.

I hurried over to see. There it was, "Talent Show Final Contestants." Sure enough, "Michael Hanlon" was printed at the very bottom. Twenty names were there. No one had been cut. Not even me.

"Congratulations," Alfred said happily. "You must have done something right."

I was thrilled in the way a guy on the gallows might be when the hangman slips a noose over his head.

As Tootles was scanning the names, he put his finger halfway down the sheet. "Cuthbert Glanville?" he said. "Our Cuthbert Glanville? What does he do?"

"Magic," I said dully. My stomach was already twisting into knots.

"Now, that I've got to see," Alfred said.

Which reminded me. The school talent shows back home were always at night, and about nobody but the kids' families ever came. But here, at Bulwick? I wouldn't be surprised if every kid had to come. Already, I feared the worst. When stage fright strikes, its effects can be legendary. If I flubbed up tomorrow as badly as I had yesterday, I'd never live it down. I turned to Tootles. "Is this something the whole school goes to? I mean, it's not required, right?"

"Oh, yes," Tootles said. "It's a huge event. Students, teachers, lots of people."

"People—you mean, like parents of the guys in the show?" I asked hopefully.

"No," Tootles said. "It's national news. Many of England's best-known entertainers began their careers on Bulwick School's Debate Room stage. Newspaper, radio and TV reporters, talent scouts, they'll all be there. The place will be packed." Tootles looked at Alf and Terrence. "Your parents are coming, right?"

They both nodded.

I watched their faces, hoping to see a wink, a smile, anything to suggest Tootles was putting me on. Neither so much as flinched.

Tootles added, "And when my father and mother hear you're in it, I'm sure they'll come, too. It's a drive from York, but I bet they'll come."

I stared at my three friends, still hoping for a sign I was being ribbed. Nothing. Finally, I said, "You know, suddenly I don't feel so hungry. Maybe I'll just skip breakfast and work on my song. I'll see you guys in class." I turned to go back to the house.

"Oh, no you don't," Alfred said, guiding me toward our table. "You must maintain proper nourishment to maintain your strength. Remember, we play Twickingham House tomorrow morning. We'll need you and your amazing throwing arm to propel us to victory. You may rehearse your song after that."

"And proper nutrition is essential for your studies," Terrance added.

"That's right," Tootles said. "Weak bodies make weak minds. Our fellow Bulwickian, Sir Winfield Stonehouse, said that—I think. If he didn't, I'm sure he would have, if there's an ounce of truth to it."

We went through the food line, but I didn't fill my tray to the danger level like I usually did. I wasn't hungry and my head hurt besides.

Saturday came and I was a nervous wreck. In the morning we beat Twickingham House, but not because of anything I did. I was awful. Not one of my throws came within ten yards of anyone wearing red-and-black stripes. Tootles actually led us with some bone-crushing tackles on their scrum half. He was taking this captain thing seriously and playing like a wild man. Alfred was practically our whole offense. Play after play, he took the ball out of scrum and found holes in the Twickingham defense. It was like he had radar. No one could stop him.

With the game over, I showered, changed, grabbed my

guitar and went straight to the practice room. I worked on the song until Tootles knocked on the door and made me go to the Trough. I ate practically nothing, a few bits of lettuce. I figured the less that goes down, the less will come up.

At six o'clock, we went back to the house to meet his parents.

Mr. Tootlington looked totally unlike Tootles. He was tall, ramrod straight and movie star handsome. He was British upper class, nobility personified. Still, for all his regal appearance, he was outgoing and friendly to all of us, especially to me. He said several times how much he was looking forward to watching my performance. All in all, he made me feel very important.

As much as Mr. Tootlington didn't look like Tootles, Mrs. Tootlington did. She was short, plump and beamed constantly. Her smile was infectious. You couldn't look at her without grinning. She just radiated cheer. Both of them were dressed like they were headed to some big deal opening night at a West End theatre instead of a high school talent show.

Alfred, Terrence and their parents came into our room and talked until it was time to go. I packed my guitar, and we walked the hundred yards or so to the Debate Room.

The place was jammed. I went backstage and found I'd be the last to perform. Tootles and the others seated themselves in the very top row, the only seats left in the whole place.

The show started and I sat, watching one act after another. After each one the place shook with applause. I was getting more nervous by the minute. My stomach was totally tied up, and I was glad I had eaten as little as I had.

About halfway through the program, Cuthbert Glanville came out. His fuzzy duck sang its song and the audience nearly came unglued. How he did it, I'll never know. But one thing I did know: He was a lock to win, which was fine by me. I just wanted to get out of this alive.

My mouth was dry as paste. I couldn't have spit if I'd wanted to. I looked around and saw the exit sign no more than twenty feet away. *It would be so easy* I thought, *just to get up and bolt.* Then I felt someone nudging my shoulder. It was the beak. I was on deck. I looked at the door, but the beak was standing in the way. I listened to my introduction.

The emcee, a Fifth Former from Ashfield House, told of my recent arrival from America and of my uncanny ability to cast an inflated pig bladder amazing distances. "We shall soon see if he can sing as well as he can play rugby," he said, which brought a good laugh from the crowd. I was glad he left out all the World Trade Center stuff and why I was at Bulwick School in the first place.

I walked to center stage and attached my guitar strap. *There, that wasn't so bad*, I thought, and I relaxed a little. A few more stomach knots loosened their grip. I swallowed hard, twice. The paste went down. I took a deep breath and looked into the front rows. Everyone appeared reasonably friendly.

I struck the first chord, a D-minor. It rang out clearly. So did the next and the next and the ones after that. As scared as I was, I don't think it showed. I opened my mouth and my voice held. The words flowed more and more easily as I told the story of Connor Flanagan, the brave lad who saved the lives of his friends that day in 1798 at Tannahill Bridge. I nailed the triple chord change in the chorus. I sang the verse that told how Connor held off a whole regiment of soldiers with nothing but a pair of pistols. I finished with the last verse where, with Connor's bullets gone, an enemy soldier had charged and shot him, point blank, through the heart. I sang the last line: Connor's final words, his cry for his country's freedom.

I struck the ending chord twice and bowed to the audience. *All right*, I thought. What a relief. I'd gotten through the whole thing without botching one word or blowing a chord. I may not have had 'em like the Logan Boys at Casey's, but at least I would be able to walk away with my head high.

I stayed bowed for a few seconds before thinking: *Something is wrong. Instead of a big ovation, there was stone cold silence. Had everyone left?* I looked up. Nope, they were still there. It flashed through my head that I had done to them what the Logans had done at Casey's–the crowd was so astounded by my brilliant performance they were unable to express their adulation.

I stared into the eyes of the first row of people. Sure enough, they looked like a herd of deer caught in headlights—and I was the truck. *Okay folks, I was good, but not that good. Come on, get off your thumbs and put your hands together.*

From the back I heard someone begin to clap. I squinted and saw that it was Tootles. A few others joined in, Alfred, Terrence and their parents. Gradually, a smattering of others added to the dismal ovation.

I felt my face burn as I hurried offstage. I threw my guitar into its case. My hands shook so bad I could barely close the latches. Then I headed for the exit.

I don't know how they got down from their seats so fast, but before I reached the door, Tootles, Terrence and Alfred had me surrounded. I looked at each of them. "Was I that bad?" I asked.

Tootles answered, "Michael, you were terrific. Your song, I'm afraid, was about as politically inappropriate as any you could possibly have chosen."

"What?" I asked. "Why's that?"

"As an American," Alf said, "you might not have known this, but Lord Tannahill is one of England's most beloved heroes, right up there with Admiral Nelson and Sir Winston Churchill. Lord Tannahill was killed that day in 1798, shot by the miserable slug in your song. Connor Flanagan is one of England's most despised villains. You might as well have sung a glowing tribute to Adolf Hitler or Osama bin Laden."

"The story is legendary," Terrence said. "During the 1790s, Lord Tannahill tried to keep Parliament from allowing Home Rule for Ireland, but not because he thought the Irish shouldn't have their independence. It was because he felt the Irish scoundrels in charge were in it only for themselves. The ultimate losers would have been the Irish themselves. Lord Tannahill had a better plan. He was about to unveil it when..."

Tootles put his hand on my shoulder and said, "It is still believed that Lord Tannahill's untimely death set the Irish cause back over two hundred years. Of course, that's not how the Rebels painted it. They made Connor Flanagan a martyr and said that Lord Tannahill had gotten what he deserved."

I stared at Tootles, my mouth open. Everything fell into place. Pearse Devlin had planned this whole thing to make me a tool of the IRA. He wanted me to learn that song so I would sing it to my friends. They would think that I sided with the Rebels—a terrorist myself. They would tell Headmaster Wilmot who would call me to his office. I'd have to tell him how I learned the song and all about my uncle's and Pearse Devlin's IRA connections. Sir John would think that if a boy like me with IRA contacts could wheedle his way into Bulwick School, the embodiment of English conservatism, then no place and no one in all of England was safe from Irish terrorists. He would have to report me to Homeland Security. I would be sent back to America or, at the very least, expelled from school. Even if allowed to stay, I'd be an outcast at Bulwick School forever.

How could Pearse Devlin have known that I would sing that song in the talent show? I wondered. It flashed through my head: That night at Casey's, talking to Mr. Devlin in the back room, Devlin must have told Uncle to have me come to Casey's that night. Devlin probably guessed that, being a Bulwick student, I knew some boys whose fathers held positions in Parliament. He may have even known about Alf's dad, Lord Noyes.

But how would he have known I'd even try out for the talent show? Then it dawned on me. He didn't. I just stepped up to the line, aimed my dart and threw a bull's-eye for him. That was my own little contribution to his devious plan.

The first weekend I could get away, if I hadn't already been kicked out of the country, I would go to Uncle's and ask Pearse Devlin why he had done this to me.

Just then, the emcee came to center stage. He held up a hand to get everyone's attention. The Debate Room quieted. He raised a sealed envelope.

"Before I announce the winner," he said, "I first want to thank this year's panel of judges, all chosen by Headmaster Wilmot for their talent show judicial experience."

At that, three people in the front row, two men and a woman, stood, turned and waved to the audience.

When the ovation subsided, the Ashfield emcee said, "And now, the moment for which you have all been waiting." He opened the envelope. He paused to read the enclosed sheet. He looked up and smiled, drawing out as long as possible his moment in the spotlight. "The 2001 Bulwick School Talent Show winner hails from Weatherby House," he said. An ear-splitting shout went up from about seventy guys in the audience. "Will you step forward and accept your award—Mr. Cuthbert Glanville." A thunderous applause followed as Cuthbert, red-faced and grinning from ear to ear, walked to center stage. He accepted the huge silver cup and bowed again to another ovation.

I stood with Tootles, Terrence and Alfred, still trying to figure out how I had gotten sucked into Pearse Devlin's plot.

Cuthbert walked shakily toward us, his face beaming. People in the audience were getting up and putting on their coats. Then, from center stage, I heard the emcee, his arms again raised, calling out loudly, "Please, may I have your attention."

It took a minute or so, but finally, people who had stood to leave sat back down. Soon, the Debate Room was quiet.

The emcee raised another envelope and said, "It a Bulwick School Talent Show rarity, but our esteemed jurists have proclaimed a secondary award, a prize for best vocalist." He opened the envelope, read it, and with much less enthusiasm, said, "They have chosen to confer this honor to Michael Hanlon."

I stared at him, blinking. Were the judges so mean-spirited as to make me face the crowd again? Why hadn't I gotten out while I could? But rather than make a scene, I walked slowly back onstage, guitar case in hand.

The Ashfield Fifth Former smiled weakly as he handed me a small silver cup. The applause, such as it was, died very quickly. I looked at the judges, then at the silent crowd and finally, again at the emcee. I realized that this might be my only chance to explain myself. "May I have a word?" I said.

He stared at me. "Are you sure you want to?" he said. I nodded. He raised his eyebrows. "It's your funeral," he whispered and stepped away.

I studied the sea of faces before me, my mind racing. Finally, I began. "First, I want to thank the judges for this award." I held the silver cup toward them. Then, hoping to break the ice, I added, "Myself, I might have gone with the duck." The three judges smiled, but not a sound came from the crowd.

Then I said, "To the rest of you I offer an apology. My friends have just told me that my song tonight comes with a controversial political message, something I knew nothing about when I first heard it last week. At that time, I was so taken by its melody and the hold it had on the audience where it was sung that I wanted to learn it right away. Not long ago someone gave me some advice. He said, 'Never sing a song in public without knowing both the song's subject and the audience for whom it is being sung.' Instead of learning more about each, I simply blundered ahead. I wish now that I had paid attention to my friend's warning."

From around the room, I heard brief chortles of ironic laughter. I looked into some nearby faces. There were a few bemused expressions, a step in the right direction.

"I think I know why I was asked to learn this song," I said.

"I promise you that its message does not, in any way, reflect my political beliefs. Again, I beg your forgiveness and thank you for not throwing something at me, as I now believe I deserved."

I turned to the emcee and nodded that I was finished. Before I could take three steps a low rumble of applause exploded into an enormous ovation. I looked up. Everyone in the entire Debate Room was on his feet, whistling and cheering.

Again, I hurried backstage. There, Tootles, Terrance and Alfred stood grinning. They looked at me as if I had just slayed a dragon. And maybe I had.

"I meant that," I said. "I'm going to talk to my uncle and his pal. They're not going to make me do what they couldn't get my father to do."

But I still didn't know exactly what that was, or what Mr. Devlin wanted from me in the first place.

Chapter Twenty-Three

It was two weeks before I got another weekend break from school. The whole time, I tried to figure out why Pearse Devlin had set me up. As it turned out, his plan was more devious and ruthless than anything I could have imagined.

That Saturday morning, I called Uncle Sean and asked him if he could pick me up. He sounded a bit put off, but finally he agreed. He came, signed me out, and we took the Kilburn Road bus back to his flat.

It was after 4 p.m. and starting to get dark, when we got there. He unlocked the door and we walked in. His suitcase stood just inside.

I saw it and asked, "Going somewhere?"

"Well, yes," he said awkwardly. "A little trip. After you called this morning, I told Mr. Devlin you were coming. He wants us to meet him at Casey's."

"Good, I'd like to see him, too," I said. "So, where are you two going?"

"Uh, well, Mr. Devlin didn't say," Uncle said, sounding flustered.

It seemed to me that Uncle Sean and Pearse Devlin had gotten awfully chummy lately. Something was going on, and I was pretty sure I was part of the reason.

Uncle grabbed his suitcase, locked the door and we walked the one block to Casey's. I followed Uncle Sean inside and looked around. The place was quiet, probably the slow time between lunch and before the after-work crowd came in. Casey greeted me with his fake twang, "Well, if it ain't our Ay-merican friend. How 'bout a hay-um sammich and a sody pop?"

"I'll pass today, Casey, but thanks," I said. I spotted Pearse Devlin sitting at a back table. He was facing two, tough-looking guys. In all the times I'd come to Casey's, I'd never seen this pair before. It looked like Pearse was giving them orders. I left Uncle Sean at the bar and went straight to Mr. Devlin.

He saw me coming and I heard him say to the two men, "Wait outside." He motioned them away with a wave of his hand. They got up, stared at me a second, then brushed past me. Without a word, they were out the door.

I looked at Mr. Devlin. "Uncle Sean says you wanted to talk to me," I said.

"Sure, sure," Mr. Devlin said. "Ah, Michael, m'boy, it's glad I am to see you. And how has Bulwick School been treatin' you?"

"Better than I deserve, considering," I said.

"Considering?" he said. He feigned surprise. "Considering what?"

"Considering a certain song I sang at the school two weeks ago," I said. "It nearly got me kicked out." I saw a faint smile cross his lips. "I think you had a reason for me to learn it. I'd like you to tell me what that was."

"What do you mean?" Pearse said, the smile vanishing. "Exactly, what are you talking about? What song do you mean?"

"You know very well," I said. "'Connor Flanagan's Stand.'"

"A fine song, it is," he said, "but I don't remember telling you to learn it."

"Mr. Devlin," I said calmly, "I think you knew that Lord Tannahill is a hero to the English people, and that his unfortunate death at the hands of an Irish rebel..."

Pearse Devlin's face went livid. "Unfortunate death, you say? Bah!" He jumped to his feet and glared down at me. "Tannahill was a bloody tyrant, he was. He kept a quarter of Ireland, all of Ulster, under his thumb for decades. Tannahill got what he deserved. The only unfortunate death that day was that of a fine young Irish lad, a patriot and a hero."

I sat before him and said as calmly as I could, "One thing I've learned about the whole Irish Rebellion thing is that there are always two sides to every story. A patriotic hero to one bunch is almost surely a murdering terrorist to the other."

"Terrorist, you say?" Pearse shouted back. "And what about your war in 1776? King George III was the same bloody tyrant we rebelled against in 1798. The same one you Americans rebelled against in your Revolution. Or am I mistaken?"

He was right. It was because Americans like George Washington, John Adams and Thomas Jefferson, living for years under intolerable British oppression, stood up to King George III that the United States of America was born. It was our ultimate victory in 1783 that gave Irish statesmen the idea that they could do the same on their soil. That's what led to the Rising of '98 and the battle at Tannahill Bridge. "All right. I won't argue that," I said.

"Then why don't you count your beloved Founding Fathers as terrorists?"

"Because the people in America were being taxed but not given any say in how they were governed," I said. "That's what started our war. We stood up for ourselves and we won."

"And the same can be said for the Irish," Pearse growled. "Are you telling me that we can't stand up for our rights?"

"I'm not saying anything of the kind," I said. "But that was two hundred years ago. This is now. The people of Ireland, Protestants and Catholics alike, are tired of the bloodshed, hatred and distrust. They've lived in the past long enough. They've got a treaty now, and they want to make it work. It would, too, but for a few people like you who keep stirring the pot and making trouble."

"Michael, my boy," Mr. Devlin said, a sneer crossing his lips, "you have tried my patience for the last time."

"What do you mean?" I said.

"Mark my words," he said. "Before this day is out, you'll be gone from my sight forever."

"What?" I said.

"You heard me," Devlin said. He leaned toward me, grabbed me by the shirt and snarled, "When your uncle told me about you, I thought you might be of some use. And you have been, but not in a way you might have wished. I'm done with you."

Mr. Devlin smirked as he got to his feet. He went to the bar and pulled Uncle Sean's arm. Uncle looked back at me. I could see fear in his eyes, but he followed Mr. Devlin to the door and into the street.

I stared at them as they left. What did Mr. Devlin mean— that he was done with me? I should have known.

Just then, the door flew open. In charged the two guys I'd seen Mr. Devlin talking to minutes before. Neither looked to be stopping by after work for a friendly pint. They came straight for me. I guessed what they had in mind.

The two men moved toward me. I looked around. I was trapped. I glanced to the bar for Casey. He wasn't there. What was going on? Casey was always behind the bar. Was he in this, too? I kept backing away from the two guys.

Then I remembered the tiny window in the loo. I turned and darted down the dark passage. I pushed open the bathroom door and jumped up to the toilet seat. I shoved the window open and squeezed my head through the space. I braced my arms on the window frame and wriggled my shoulders and then my hips through the hole.

I was just about out when someone grabbed my left ankle. I

kicked back. My heel hit something—hard. The next thing I heard was a blood-curdling scream. My foot came free and I pulled myself the rest of the way through the window.

I fell awkwardly, dropping six feet and slamming my head on the cement. I rolled groggily to my feet, wasting several precious seconds. I glanced in both directions and saw light at one end of the alley. I ran for it. In front of me was a street with lots of traffic. I had to get to it before Devlin's goons did. I was almost there when they charged into the alley. They stopped short and stared directly at me. I was trapped—this time for sure. I froze.

The two thugs moved toward me, preparing to finish their job. The bigger man, holding a blood-soaked towel to his face, snarled angrily as he led the way. In his right hand he waved a three-foot-long tire iron.

A moment later, as if two guys weren't enough, a third man stepped into the alley behind them. The man with the bloody nose and the iron bar charged, his weapon raised. The third man raced down the alley toward him. He pulled a small club from his hip pocket and smashed it into the guy's skull. The goon with the bloody nose dropped like a stone. The second man spun around, surprised, and the new guy whacked him on the head. Both of Devlin's men lay in the alley, down for the count.

I stared at my rescuer. I said weakly, "Thanks. You saved me. Who are you?"

"A friend of your uncle's," he answered. "I'm a Provo, like him."

"A Provo?" I asked. I tried to remember what a Provo was. It seemed like that's what Dad was, and Uncle, too. Also, Pearse and his two henchmen.

"Aye," he said.

I said, "So's Pearse Devlin."

"Pearse Devlin *was* a Provo," he said. "But now he's IFI Your Uncle wouldn't listen to me when I tried to tell him."

I had no idea what IFI meant, but I wasn't about to argue with the guy. I mean, he'd just saved my life. I waited a second, looking confused, and asked, "What's the I-F…whatever you said?"

"They were good IRA men once," the man said, "but now they're nothing but a bunch of gangsters. Take my advice: Get out of this part of London, and don't expect any help from your uncle." The man pocketed his club and moved quickly toward the Kilburn Road.

I took one look at the two thugs sprawled out at my feet. They were showing signs of coming to. I stepped around them and ran to the street. When I got there I saw a bus pulling away from the curb. I raced toward its rear boarding platform. As I was about to grab the handle, the driver sped up. I lunged for the grip but missed it by an inch.

I stumbled, lost balance and knew I could not regain it. Instead, I ducked my head, rolled once on the street and bounced to my feet. I looked back and saw Devlin's men, charging out of the alley. They saw me and raced in my direction.

I knew I couldn't outrun them, not very far at least, so I headed for Uncle's place. It was less than a block away. If I could get in, I'd be okay. I was almost there when I remembered he'd locked the door as we left for Casey's. I glanced behind me and saw Devlin's thugs. They were maybe a hundred yards back and coming fast.

It was then that I thought of Felicity Brown. She was my only hope. I ran across the street and up to her door. I turned the knob and pushed my way in.

There she was, sitting at a table, holding a book. She jumped to her feet and stared at me, scared out of her wits. Then her expression changed.

"It's you!" she said. "Michael, what's going on?"

"Two guys are after me!" I said, catching my breath.

"You've got to hide me. Get me out of here."

Felicity ran to the front door. She looked outside. In one motion she slammed the door and slid the deadbolt into place. Just then, the first guy hit the steps.

"There's a back alley," she said. She grabbed my arm and pulled me along a short hall. "Who are they?"

"My uncle got mixed up with some really bad guys," I said. "Now they're after me."

"Right," she said. "There's a back door."

In about four strides we made our way to the kitchen. I looked through a window and saw the second guy charging down the alley. He was coming hard for us. Felicity saw him and threw that bolt shut too.

The two men started beating hard on each of the doors. I knew the locks wouldn't hold for long. "Call the police," I said.

"No time," she said. "Our only hope is through the roof. Come on."

We ran to what looked like a closet door. She pulled it open and shoved me ahead. I found myself in a two-by-two-foot shaft. I looked up and saw no light.

She slammed the door. It was instantly black. "Go," she said. I felt a metal rung in front of me. "Hurry," she said. "They've broken the doors in. They'll find us any second."

I grabbed the first rung and then the next. I went straight up as fast as I could. Felicity was right behind me. I hit my head on something. "Ow," I screamed.

"Undo the latch!" she yelled. I felt for a hook, found it, and in the instant before I shoved the square lid away, light from below flooded the shaft. "Hurry," she yelled. "Get on the roof."

I threw open the square cover and pushed it aside. I scrambled through the opening. She was beside me in a second. She picked up the lid, turned it sideways, and dropped it down the hole. A second later I heard a shriek and then a stream of obscenities.

"That won't stop them for long," Felicity said. I followed her as she ran along the roof to the edge of the building. "Here's the fire escape," she said.

She got to it first and I was right behind. In seconds we were on the pavement and running for the Kendal Street Station, the tube stop where Uncle and I had landed on my first day in London. She ran past the ticket booth, jumped the turnstiles and flew down the stairs to the train platform. I raced to catch up with her. She was thirty feet ahead and charging into a crowd of passengers who were pouring out of the train and coming our way.

I dodged them and kept my eye on Felicity as she bolted to the front car. The door was open and we jumped aboard.

"Think we lost 'em?" I asked hopefully, gasping for breath.

Her eyes flashed back to the loading dock. Just then I heard a mechanical voice say, "Mind the gap."

The doors were closing when I saw the two men dart down the stairs and dash for the train.

"That's them," she said. "If they get on, it'll be in the last car. They'll work their way forward until they find us. We'll have to get off at the next stop."

The train was at full speed in seconds. Less than a minute later, it was slowing to a halt.

"Here's what we do," she said. "We wait by the open door. I'll watch to see if they get off. If they don't, we'll have to get out. As the door is closing, we'll jump off. You've got to be quick. If you get caught in the door, you'll be dragged under the car and crushed under the wheels. Got it?"

"Yeah, I got it," I said.

"Once we're off, as the cars go by, we'll watch to see if your pals are still aboard. If they are, we're safe. If we don't see them, then we've got to hide here until we're sure they've left the station."

Several seconds passed as more passengers boarded.

I stared seriously at Felicity. "I've gotten you into some real danger," I said. "Even if I get away, they still know where you live."

"Aye, Love, I've thought of that," she said. "But they're after you, not me. Right now we've got to make sure we've lost them."

The train screeched to a halt. The doors opened and passengers moved off the train. We stood at the door watching to see if Devlin's thugs had gotten out. New passengers poured on. The mechanical voice once again said, "Mind the gap."

"Get ready," Felicity said. She pulled me toward the open door. When it started to close she jumped. I was right behind, but not close enough. The door caught my shoulder. I panicked for a second but pulled my arm free. I fell to the station platform, got up and looked for Felicity. She was ahead of me, waving me toward her. "Get behind this trash bin," she said. "We'll watch the cars from here."

The engine started. In seconds the train was moving. In the car next to the one we'd been in I saw the guy with the bloody nose. He was making his way to the front of the train.

"That's him," I said.

"Aye," Felicity said. "And I think I saw the other bloke, too. We're okay for now, but we still have to get you back to school before they decide to come for you there. I've got a cabbie friend who uses this station to wait for fares."

This time she took my hand in hers. She squeezed it warmly and we walked up the stairs to the street. It was late afternoon and dark when we got to the cabstand. Her friend was there and they talked for less than a minute. She nodded to me, and we slid into the back seat.

I relaxed for the first time in what seemed like hours. "I don't know what I'd have done if you hadn't been home," I said. "Those guys trashed your place looking for me. What if they come back to get you?"

"Let's get you to Bulwick," Felicity said. "I can take care of myself."

I looked at her in wonder. I smiled and said, "I don't doubt that one bit."

Chapter Twenty-Four

It was pitch dark, close to nine o'clock, when the cab pulled up to Weatherby House. I reached to open the car door, but Felicity grabbed my hand. "Hold on," she said. "We've got to make sure those goons didn't beat us here." She hopped out, walked around the cab, and then looked in every direction. She climbed back in and sat down. She smiled her dazzling smile, wrapped her arms around me and planted her lips on mine.

It was like nothing I had ever felt in my entire life. It jolted me, shook my entire being. Mom had kissed me before, you know, like moms do, a peck on the cheek. This was nothing like that. I pulled her toward me and kissed back, thinking I never wanted to let go. She smiled, lifted the door handle and pushed it open. "I'll see you," she said. She looked into my eyes and nudged me into the street.

I stood on the sidewalk and watched as she waved goodbye. The cabbie hit the gas. Felicity was gone.

I ran up to my room, walked in, and found Tootles, sitting at his desk. His glasses were perched on his head and he was rubbing his eyes. He looked up. His face was red. He looked sick. When he recognized me, his jaw dropped.

"What's wrong?" I asked.

"Is that really you?" he said.

"Yeah, of course," I said. "You were expecting someone else?"

"I might have expected anyone but you," he said. "Sir John told us you'd quit school. He said you were already on a plane back to America."

"What made him think that?" I asked.

"He said your uncle called. Your money is gone and he couldn't be your guardian any more. He said a friend of his scraped up enough cash to get you a ticket back to New York. Your uncle told Sir John that it would be best for you."

I turned and saw Terrence and Alfred at the door. They looked surprised to see me, too. Alf said, "Your uncle told Sir John that that's what you wanted—that you wanted to go home."

"Uncle was lying," I said.

"So, you're not leaving?" Tootles asked.

"Eventually, I guess. I suppose I'll have to, but it's not what I want," I said. "Hey, I don't have a lot to say about it. My uncle's buddy thinks I'm already on the plane, but I gave his goons the slip."

"Who are you talking about?" Tootles asked. "What goons? What's going on?"

I told Tootles how I got away at Casey's, slipped through the loo window, and then ran like crazy and broke into Felicity Brown's front door. I made a long story short. "They're probably still out there looking for me," I said. "When they find me, they'll put me on the plane for sure."

"So, you really don't want to leave?" Tootles asked.

"No, of course not," I said, "but I don't think I have a choice."

Tootles stared at me for a second. Then he said, "I've got an idea. Look, it's almost time for lights out. You boys, get some sleep. Michael, don't go anywhere. Keep this door locked." He turned and grabbed his coat. "If those two blokes show up, don't let them in."

"Trust me," I said. "A locked door means nothing to them."

182

Tootles turned to Alfred and Terrence. "Then you boys have to listen for them," he said. "If someone tries to break in, get Mr. Epping." He went for the door.

"Where are you going?" I asked, but Tootles was already down the hall, heading for the stairs.

Alfred, Terrence and I watched from our window as Tootles crossed the High Street and disappeared through Sir John's front door. We waited for an hour, but when nobody came and I couldn't keep my eyes open another minute, I hit the hay. Terrence and Alfred went to their room and did the same. As they left, I did as Tootles said and locked the door.

I still had no idea what Tootles was doing or where he was going.

Next morning, the sun broke through my window. I heard a knock at the door and nearly jumped out of my shorts. "Who's there?" I shouted.

"It's me," Tootles said. "My father's here. Did those two blokes ever show?"

"No," I said. I turned the lock and opened the door. Tootles stared urgently at me. He was still wearing the same clothes he'd had on the night before.

His father stood behind him, tall and straight as ever. He smiled at me and said, "Walter came home last night with a most alarming story. I'd like to hear it from you."

"Well, it's kind of long," I said. "It starts before I was born, when my mom and dad lived in Belfast."

He looked surprised. "Your parents are from Northern Ireland?" he asked.

I nodded. "Yeah, like I said—it goes back a ways."

"Then definitely, that's where I want you to start," he said.

He listened as I told him my story, from how Mom and Dad met, why they left Ireland and about their jobs in the Twin Towers, all the way up to the part where I met Devlin.

Mr. Tootlington blinked. He held up his hand. "Devlin, you say? Might that have been a Mr. Pearse Devlin?" he asked.

"Yeah," I said. I was surprised Mr. Tootlington would know anything about someone in the IRA, I mean, talk about polar opposites.

"Can you describe this Mr. Devlin?" Mr. Tootlington asked calmly.

"Yeah," I said. "He's stocky, medium height, strong, maybe forty years old. I guess he belongs to one of those IRA splinter groups. I met him at a pub called Casey's near my uncle's place. Everyone, even Casey, treated him like he was a really big deal."

"Hold on," Mr. Tootlington said. He took a phone from his vest and punched one number. "Townsend, this is Tootlington," he said. "Tell me if you know the whereabouts of Pearse Devlin." He paused. "Yes, of Belfast. Also, a Mr. Sean Hanlon. They may be working here in London."

Mr. Tootlington listened, and then said, "I see. Can you bring them to Scotland Yard?" He listened. "Fine, how soon can you be there?" "Thank you, Tom, I'll meet you in an hour."

"What's going on?" I asked.

"Seems both your uncle and Mr. Devlin were detained last night at Heathrow Airport," Mr. Tootlington said. "British Customs found an envelope with papers that had your signature on them. The officers were suspicious of some illegal activity and placed the two men in custody. They were about to release them for lack of evidence when I called. They should be at the Yard in an hour."

I thought back, and then shook my head. "I never signed any papers," I said.

"I don't doubt that," Mr. Tootlington said, "but do you remember seeing any bank notes or certificates of deposit made in your name?"

"No, but I do remember, back in New York as we were packing for London Uncle Sean putting a thick envelope in his suitcase. It didn't mean anything to me, but that might be what you're talking about."

"Has your uncle ever seen your signature?" Mr. Tootlington asked.

"No, not that I can think of," I said. I thought for a moment. "Wait, sure, it's on my passport. He'd have seen that."

"And your passport is here?"

"It is now," I said, going to the top drawer of my dresser. I got it out and showed it to him. "But until I came to Bulwick School, I kept it at his place."

"So, he or Mr. Devlin could have forged your signature on those documents," Mr. Tootlington said thoughtfully. "Do you think that's possible?"

"A few days ago, I wouldn't have believed it," I said, "but now it makes perfect sense. From what Sir John said to Tootles, I think Mr. Devlin was planning on sending me back to the United States. Yesterday afternoon, two guys had me trapped at Casey's Pub and were going to grab me. I took off running, but they were right behind me. I went to a friend's house, a girl by the name of Felicity Brown. She's the one who really got me out of there. The two guys broke down her doors, front and back, and probably trashed her house. She got me to a subway and we ditched them there. I can't believe how lucky I was."

"You may be luckier than you think," Mr. Tootlington said. "Without a passport, you'd never have boarded any plane, much less one to the United States. I believe Mr. Devlin's men had other, more permanent intentions for you."

I suddenly realized what he meant. "I didn't think about

that," I said.

"All right," Mr. Tootlington said, getting to his feet. "Let's go to Scotland Yard. We'll see what your uncle and Mr. Devlin have to say for themselves."

"Me, too?" Tootles asked eagerly. "Can I come?"

"I'm afraid not, Walter." Mr. Tootlington said. "But I'll ask Michael to assist me. Is that all right with you, Michael?"

"Sure," I said quickly. "I don't think I'll be able to stay here at Bulwick much longer anyway. I've got a feeling all my school money is gone. I can't believe Uncle Sean would do this, but I wouldn't put it past Pearse Devlin."

"We'll see," Mr. Tootlington said. "I hope, for your sake, as well as your uncle's, that he can prove his innocence."

Mr. Tootlington and I went down the front stairs of Weatherby House into a brilliant morning. At the High Street curb, a long, black Rolls Royce was parked with its motor running. A man in a green uniform, chauffeur I guessed, stood beside it. He opened the door for Mr. Tootlington and then moved around to let me in. He then got in the passenger seat next to the driver, also wearing green. The car pulled away.

A thick window separated Mr. Tootlington and me from the front seat. Tootles' dad pressed a button. A glass partition slid down. "Scotland Yard, please," Mr. Tootlington said. He pressed the button again, closing the window. He turned to me and said, "You may speak freely. This compartment is soundproof and checked daily for concealed surveillance devices. I'm very curious about this. Tell me about the song you sang at the talent show. Where did you learn it?"

"'Connor Flanagan's Stand?'" I said. "That's another long story."

"We have time," Mr. Tootlington said.

"All right," I said. I wondered where to begin. I drew in a long breath, "When I first came to England, Uncle Sean and I had been eating at a little place called Casey's, the pub I told you about. Every night, a few people would come in, play guitars and sing, mostly Irish songs. It was fun and I was learning a lot about Ireland and England, all about the Troubles.

"One night Mr. Devlin showed up. It was a couple of days after Uncle Sean had lashed out at Sir John. Uncle had asked Mr. Devlin if he could help me. Anyway, Pearse came into Casey's that night and told me he might be able to pull some strings to get me into Bulwick School. I told him that if I couldn't get in on my own, I'd rather go someplace else. As it turned out, I was accepted without his help. But a few weeks later, I was at Casey's again and Mr. Devlin took me to the back room. He started asking me questions about how I was doing at school. He said he'd heard me sing a few times. He said he wanted me to learn a song."

Mr. Tootlington stopped me there and asked, "At any time, did you ever mention my name?"

I was about to say no when I remembered the grilling Devlin had given me before telling me about the song. "Well, not exactly," I said. "He wanted to know who I knew at school, and I told him about my three best friends. He didn't seem to care about Terrence or Alf, you know, the guys across the hall, but he peppered me with questions about Tootles."

"How do you mean?" he asked.

"Well, when I told him my roommate's name was Tootles, he said, 'Tootles?' And I said, 'Yeah, Walter Tootlington–Tootles, for short.' He asked me what I knew about you, if you were in the House of Lords. I told him no, but that Alf's dad, Lord Noyes, might be. I remember Mr. Devlin smiling, sort of to himself, like I'd told him something he really wanted to know. Suddenly, Mr. Devlin stopped asking me questions about Tootles and started to talk about the song he wanted me to learn."

Mr. Tootlington nodded thoughtfully. "I take it the song

was the one you sang at the show."

"That's right," I said. "What an idiot I was. I should have known better. Uncle told me never to sing about anything Irish, how songs like that could get me in trouble. But I figured I was at school. It wasn't like I was at Casey's where people get all crazy about political stuff. Also, I figured the song was so old no one would know what it was about, not that I really knew myself. I just liked the tune. For sure, I didn't know everything Tootles clued me in on after I'd sung it at the talent show. Man, I could have been kicked out of school. So ever since then, I've been trying to figure out why Devlin set me up like that. I mean, I figured since he'd been friends with my dad, I could trust him. I was dead wrong about that, too. Last night, I think I found out what he was up to, but I'm still not sure. Some of it still doesn't make sense."

Just then, the car came to a stop in front of a modern glass and steel building. The sign read, "New Scotland Yard." It was not the Scotland Yard I'd expected, you know, ivy covered walls, drawbridges and spiraling turrets.

I followed Mr. Tootlington inside. Inch-thick, bulletproof glass was everywhere. People scurried about or stared into computer screens. They looked like they were working under a bomb threat, which, come to think of it, they might have been.

We stopped in front of a uniformed man sitting on the other side of a glass wall. He looked up casually. Suddenly, his eyes bulged. He jumped to his feet and pushed a button. I heard a buzz, then a click. Another man hurried to a steel door and opened it. He bowed to Mr. Tootlington, which I thought was strange. I figured he had Tootles' dad mixed up with someone else, some kind of big deal official. We walked into another room.

Two men in black suits stood there. Uncle Sean was sitting in a corner. He didn't look up, didn't even see me. He just stared at the floor. Pearse Devlin sat beside him, looking fit to be tied, which, I guess, he was. Both were in handcuffs. When Pearse saw me he blurted out, "How in...?"

At that, Uncle Sean's eyes shot in my direction. His face brightened with a look of relief. Then he frowned and stared back at the floor. Not so with Mr. Devlin. He glared at me, his jaw tightening, threatening.

The two men in suits introduced themselves very formally. The first was Constable Barnett and the other was Sergeant Johnson. Just then, a third man came in carrying a thick envelope. He was older than the others and wore a uniform with lots of gold braid. He held his hand out to me and said he was Chief Superintendent Townsend, head of homeland security, and that he was in charge of this case.

He may have been in charge, but he was the cheeriest-looking person I have ever met, except maybe for Tootles' mom. His red face bubbled, and he smiled as he shook my hand. He made a slight bow to Mr. Tootlington and even shook hands with Uncle Sean and Pearse Devlin, although that was a bit awkward with the handcuffs.

Looking at Uncle Sean and Mr. Devlin, Chief Townsend said pleasantly, "Good morning, gentlemen. I hope we can have this matter cleared up quickly, and you can be on your way."

At that, I saw Pearse Devlin smile. A relieved look crossed Uncle's face.

Chief Townsend looked at Uncle Sean and then Mr. Devlin. "First," Chief Townsend said, "if you could tell us why you were at Heathrow Airport holding these papers?" At that, he opened the folder.

Uncle Sean stared at the packet and then at Mr. Devlin. Pearse eyed Uncle Sean and shook his head like, "Don't answer that." I watched Uncle Sean, hoping he'd see me, but he turned his gaze back to the floor.

Pearse Devlin's jaw jutted out. He demanded, "I want my lawyer."

"There will be time for that," Chief Townsend said easily.

"Secondly, you were each holding tickets for a flight to Belfast. Can you tell me your reason for going there?"

Still, Uncle Sean said nothing, but Devlin said, "I was just going to visit me mum."

"Oh, well, then. That's very good," Chief Townsend said happily. "So, I suppose we can turn our questions to this other fellow, uh, Mr. Hanlon, is that right?" Uncle Sean's eyes widened. He glanced at Mr. Devlin, then back to the inspector.

Devlin moved to get up, but Chief Townsend gently held him down with a hand on his shoulder.

"So, Mr. Hanlon," the chief continued, "I'm told you were the one carrying this envelope when you and Mr. Devlin were boarding the plane." He showed a gold-embossed certificate to everyone in the room. It was a trust fund in the sum of $30,000 from Rotary International. I looked at it and saw that it was made out to me, but that I couldn't cash it until I turned eighteen. My signature was at the bottom along with a copy of my birth certificate. It showed that I was eighteen, not fourteen. It looked real.

Chief Townsend then took several receipt stubs and showed them to the others. Each was made out to me for different sums of money. All had been signed over to the Benevolent Society for the Sisters of St. Patrick's Cathedral.

He turned to me and said, "I see that you have a strong interest in this religious group. That's very generous of you, Michael. I'm sure you've determined it a worthy cause. If my calculations are correct, these receipts total over two million US dollars. That would go a long way to aid the Sisters' beneficiaries. Were you aware that the money given to you was being used in this way?"

I gulped as I stared at the receipts. "No, sir," I said. I looked at Uncle Sean, but he still wouldn't meet my gaze.

"All but this one last Rotary International Certificate of

Deposit," Chief Townsend continued. He again showed me the gilt-embossed document. "It is the only such instrument not yet negotiated. Michael, is that your signature at the bottom?"

I studied it carefully. "It looks like it," I said, "but I didn't sign it."

"So, as with all these other contributions that were supposed to pay for your education, it appears that this too, was about to be donated to the so-called Sisters' Relief Fund. Are you aware, Michael, that this fund is, in fact, a front for the IRA splinter organization known as the IFI, Ireland For Irish, and that your money was being used for purposes other than the Sisters' good works?"

I glared at Pearse Devlin. He looked back with a sneer.

Just then, Uncle Sean blurted out, "No, it's not like that, Michael. You have to believe me. I didn't know. Pearse told me he was just borrowing the money. He said you'd get it back when you needed it. He said..."

"Shut up, you fool," Devlin blurted. He turned to Chief Townsend. "I'm not saying another word until I see my lawyer. Get me a phone, now."

Chief Townsend turned to Constable Barnett and said, "Bryan, please escort Mr. Devlin down the hall and allow him use of the telephone. In the meantime, I have a few more questions for Mr. Hanlon."

As Pearse Devlin moved to the door he turned to Uncle Sean. "You keep your mouth shut, Sean. Not another word, do you hear? You're in this as deep as I am."

Uncle Sean nodded, fear and confusion in his eyes. When Pearse left the room and the door was shut, Uncle Sean turned to me and said, "Don't you see, Michael? I was doing it for you. Mr. Devlin told me he was going to use your money to help the Cause, to unify Ireland. You'd be a hero, just like your dad. Mr. Devlin said you'd help put an end to our most hated enemy. He wanted to finish what Connor Flanagan had started at Tannahill Bridge in 1798. He wanted to end the Tannahill family line forever. Don't you know who wrote that song?"

I shook my head. "No," I said. "It's two hundred years old, even Dominic Logan didn't know."

"It's not two hundred years old," Uncle Sean said. "Your father wrote it and sang it for the first time twenty-five years ago. It was that night in Newry, the night one of our men gunned down the British soldier. Our whole family was murdered the next morning—except for Brendan and me. Brendan had written it only a week before. He sang it that night to incite the troops and to honor the memory of one of our own family."

I looked at Uncle Sean, almost afraid to ask. "One of our own family?"

"Sure," Uncle said. "Connor Flanagan himself. He was your great-great-great-grand uncle. Mr. Devlin knew this because he was with Brendan when your dad wrote the song. Devlin thought, if you knew the truth, you wouldn't sing it for your friends, and then Tootles wouldn't tell his dad. But if you sang it for your friends, word would get out and you'd be linked to the IRA. Your friends would warn Sir John, and that would flush Mr. Tootlington into the open. Tootlington would come for Mr. Devlin, and Devlin would kill him, maybe even get Tootles, too. He said that would finish what Connor started." He looked at me like he couldn't believe I didn't get it.

I returned the stare. I was dumbstruck. I got it, but I couldn't believe it.

"Remember that night at Casey's?" he asked. "The night I picked you up from school?"

I nodded. I remembered how strange it was that Uncle Sean suddenly wanted to see me after so much time.

"Well, I didn't tell you the real reason why I called you," Uncle said. "Mr. Devlin told me he wanted to talk to you. He'd heard you were rooming with a boy called Tootles, and he wanted to make sure who it was. He'd guessed that the boy was Walter Tootlington, the son of George Tootlington. If that was true, Devlin wanted to make sure that you heard your dad's song. He said to make sure not to tell you the full story, who wrote it and why—what happened after your dad sang it at Newry. He figured that once you heard the song, knowing how you are about folk music, that you'd want to learn it. He knew all about the Bulwick School talent contest, what a big deal it was. He hoped you'd be picked and then sing it for the show."

I stared at Uncle Sean. So, I *had* been right. Pearse Devlin *had* set me up. I was betrayed by my own uncle. I felt woozy like I had on September 11th when the Twin Towers and my whole world collapsed.

Uncle Sean pointed to the envelope still in Chief Townsend's hand. "I gave your money to Mr. Devlin because he told me it was for the Cause. It wasn't until last night that I found out that his cause wasn't to help unify Ireland, but for his own gambling and drug rings. He said if I told the police, he'd kill me, and you, too. He said if I kept quiet he'd let you live, put you on a plane and send you back to America. Now I wonder if that wasn't a lie, too."

I looked at Uncle Sean. "That doesn't make any sense," I said. "Why did Devlin want to kill Mr. Tootlington, or Tootles even? Tootles is just a regular kid!"

"Haven't you figured out who this man is?" Uncle answered, nodding to Mr. Tootlington.

"Yeah, he's my best friend's dad," I said. "So what?"

Before he could answer, Chief Townsend spoke. "I believe we've heard enough, Mr. Hanlon. I have no choice now but to charge you with supporting a terrorist conspiracy to assassinate a House of Lords member. Both you and Mr. Devlin will be tried for high treason. Your confession is quite valid and has been witnessed by no fewer than three British citizens, including Lord

Tootlington himself."

What? I thought. *Lord Tootlington?*

"Take Mr. Hanlon away, Peter," Chief Townsend said.

Lieutenant Johnson stepped forward and put his hand on Uncle Sean's arm. As he went through the door, Uncle looked at me sadly and said, "You have to believe me, Michael. I never meant for this to happen. I didn't know."

At that, the door closed behind him.

Chapter Twenty-Five

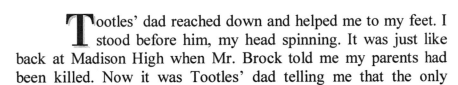

Tootles' dad reached down and helped me to my feet. I stood before him, my head spinning. It was just like back at Madison High when Mr. Brock told me my parents had been killed. Now it was Tootles' dad telling me that the only family I had left, Uncle Sean, was going to jail. Maybe forever. I was now totally, completely and utterly alone.

"I will take you back to school," Lord Tootlington said. "We'll talk in the car."

The black Rolls pulled up to the curb. The man in the uniform came around and opened our doors. It was then that I noticed: This wasn't a chauffeur's outfit. It was a military uniform. My friend's father was a much bigger deal than I thought.

We got in and Tootles' dad lowered the window between himself and the driver. "Bulwick School, please. Weatherby House," he said. The man nodded and Lord Tootlington raised the glass shield.

I sat in my seat, dread setting in. "What am I going to do?" I asked miserably. "I've got nothing: no family, no home, no money."

"That's what I want to talk to you about," he said.

"What's there to say?" I asked.

"Actually, quite a bit," Lord Tootlington said. "First, I want you to get your chin up. There is an old saying: When one door closes, another opens. Come now, chin up."

I took a deep breath, raised my head and looked him in the eye.

"Jolly good," he said. "Now we can talk. How would you like to begin?"

"Maybe with a question," I said.

"Of course," he answered.

"The policeman back there called you *Lord* Tootlington," I said. "I've known Tootles for almost three months. I mean, we talk about Alfred's dad being some sort of earl, but nothing about you being anything like that. Are you really a lord?"

"Yes," he said. "My full name is Lord George Tannahill Tootlington, Sixth Earl of Dungannon. And, although I don't display my title in public, it is nothing for which I am ashamed."

"Why would you even worry about that?" I asked.

"It's complicated," Lord Tootlington said. "Alfred Noyes' father has a somewhat different circumstance than I do. He is an earl, but he's not a voting member of the House of Lords. That is, his role is largely social."

"I don't understand," I said. "How many kinds of lords are there?"

"A few," he said. "My position carries an often perilous Parliamentary duty. I have been the Anti-terrorism Committee chairman for the House of Lords for twenty years. The men of our family have long embraced the responsibility of rooting out and capturing those who threaten our country from within—spies, terrorists—that sort. We have done this since the day Connor Flanagan killed Lord Tannahill in 1798. Over the years, Irish rebels have assassinated not only Lord Tannahill, but also my father, my grandfather and my great-grandfather."

I blinked in disbelief. "Let me make sure I've got this right," I said. "Do you mean to tell me that Lord Tannahill, the guy in my father's song, is your ancestor?"

"That is correct," Lord Tootlington said. "Our family peerage in Ulster is a very old one. King Henry VIII granted the first Lord Tootlington a vast estate in Ulster in the 1500s. For centuries my forefathers protected the king's land as they were instructed. In hindsight, their methods were often cruel and unfair. Regrettably, horrible atrocities and reprisals on both sides led to four hundred years of hostility. That's water under the bridge. It is now my aim to rectify the wrongs my family has brought upon the Irish people and to bring lasting harmony. We believe we are on the right track with the Good Friday Peace Treaty. Unfortunately, there are a few individuals, people like Pearse Devlin, who continue to promote hatred and violence. I believe they do it for their own self-serving interests."

"Tootles never told me anything about his family at all," I said.

"Nor should he have," Lord Tootlington said. "Walter understands the risk his surname carries with it. For years, my work in Parliament dealt mostly with the 'Irish Question,' as the centuries-old unrest has come to be called. Recently, my role has grown to include defending Great Britain against worldwide terrorists. The al-Qaeda organization is every bit as active in England as it is in the United States. They have made numerous attempts on my life: car bombs, sniper attacks, arson. It is for my family's safety that I do not make public anything of my personal life."

He looked at me and continued, "I asked you to come with me to Scotland Yard for a reason. I hoped you could help me with a case I've been working on for several years. This morning when you mentioned Pearse Devlin's name, I understood what he was doing. It is a shame your uncle was drawn into the man's plot. I believe Mr. Hanlon was only trying to help his people in the best way he could, but Mr. Devlin's case is a far different matter."

"He's in the IFI," I said. "Is that what you mean?"

"He's its organizer and leader," Lord Tootlington said. "The IFI was once just another Rebel splinter group, perhaps more militant than the others. But since the Good Friday Treaty, most of its members changed their allegiance to other factions. That left only a few hardcore thugs, Devlin at the top, and they devolved into a band of criminals, drug peddlers, and racketeers. Today, without your help and your uncle's testimony, Mr. Devlin might again have slipped through my fingers, as he has so often in the past. But, by your coming with me to Scotland Yard, your uncle recognized Mr. Devlin's plan. He confessed to his part in it, knowing it was the only way to put Mr. Devlin in prison for good."

"I can't believe Uncle Sean didn't see through Pearse's scheme," I said.

"As you said yourself, Pearse Devlin is a devious man, as cunning as he is unscrupulous," Lord Tootlington said. "His IFI gang took to terrorizing honest citizens of all stripes: Catholic, Protestant, Irish and English. To describe Pearse Devlin as a terrorist or anarchist is too kind. Those terms suggest, at least to their countrymen, a higher purpose, treacherous and cruel as they may be to the rest of the civilized world. No, Mr. Devlin is simply a criminal. You may rest assured that your uncle's testimony will put him behind bars forever. Knowing your uncle's minor role, I will do what I can to lighten his sentence. He did, however, assist in a treasonous act, so he will go to prison. In this present political climate, British citizens will not be willing to ignore his role, small as it was."

I stared at Lord Tootlington for a moment, and then asked, "With my uncle in jail, what am I going to do?"

Lord Tootlington sat back in his seat. "Ordinarily, since you are a minor, you would be deported to your homeland and become subject to its social welfare system. Likely, you would be placed in a foster care facility."

"Right," I said. "Sort of like an orphanage."

"It goes by another name now," Lord Tootlington said, "but yes, that's what it is."

"I've known kids who've lived in foster homes," I said. "It can be pretty rough."

"Yes," Lord Tootlington said. "But in the end, it may be better than the alternative, which is, by no means, an entirely safe option."

He seemed to be offering a way out. "An option?" I asked.

"Yes," Lord Tootlington said. "There is one other possibility."

"Everything sounds pretty cut and dried," I said. "My uncle goes to jail. I go to the United States and live in a foster home. What else is there?"

Just then, Lord Tootlington's phone buzzed. He held up his hand to me and took the call.

Lord Tootlington spoke for several minutes on his phone. When he clicked off, I said. "You said something about a choice."

"Yes," he said, "but I'm almost afraid to suggest it."

"Why's that?" I asked.

"Because of how it might affect your safety. It could put you in a position of extreme danger," he said.

"And why would that be?" I asked. "What could be worse than living in some orphanage?"

Lord Tootlington looked me in the eye. "I have the authority, as Earl of Dungannon, to harbor you for a time under my care. Officially, you would be my ward. As such, you would remain in England until your eighteenth birthday and continue at Bulwick School through graduation."

I stared at Lord Tootlington. "My money is gone," I said. "I couldn't afford that."

"I would pay your expenses," he said simply.

I knew I couldn't be hearing him right. "You would put me through nearly five years at Bulwick School?"

He nodded. "My main concern is the danger you might face. For my part, I am willing to consider it for several reasons. First, I am indebted to you for assisting me in Pearse Devlin's capture, a known threat to Britain's security. Also, and you may not be aware of this, you have become a trusted companion to the Viscount of Dungannon."

"I am?" I asked. I'd never met a viscount and had no idea where Dungannon was. "Who's that?"

"You know him better as Tootles," Lord Tootlington said.

"Tootles is a viscount?" I said. "Look, I'm not real clear on all this title stuff. Tootles never said anything about it to me or anyone else as far as I know."

"Walter has learned to be discreet," Lord Tootlington said. "You would be the only one at Bulwick School besides Sir John to know."

I decided to get back to the point. "You said that what you were offering could be risky," I said. "Being in charge of the anti-terror group is your job. Why would I be in danger?"

"Terrorists are a merciless bunch," Lord Tootlington said. "They will use any means to achieve their goals. To them, I am an obstacle in their path. Their primary objective is to force me to bend to their will. A common tactic to that end is to abduct someone from my family. Should you accept my offer, you would be included as a member. Walter has been taught the methods terrorists use to lure him into a trap. But you have never lived under those conditions. Britain's enemies will consider you an easy target to get to me."

"I see what you mean," I said. "I couldn't go anywhere without the chance someone might grab me and hold me for ransom, or kill me at some maniac's whim."

"That's right," Lord Tootlington said.

I sat back in the soft leather car seat. "Pearse Devlin almost got away with it, didn't he," I said. "Now I know why you've been after him so long. He is one evil dude. I fell right into his trap by singing the Connor Flanagan song. I wish I'd let Tootles hear it before doing it in front of the entire school. He would have stopped me right then."

"Yes, he may have," Lord Tootlington said. "But if you hadn't performed that song at the concert, I would not have become alerted to a possible threat. Also, as a consequence, you would not have confronted Mr. Devlin at Casey's last night. He would not have tried to abduct you, and I would not have brought him to justice."

I nodded. "You know, you're a lot like Tootles. He's always looking on the bright side. I don't see how he does it, knowing the danger he's always in."

"Walter is stronger than his image might portray," Lord Tootlington said.

"I'm sure of that," I said, remembering how he stood up to Billy Monmouth that day in September and how he never backed down from guys twice his size in rugby games. "So, why did you let Tootles come to Bulwick School where he might meet all sorts of people, including me, who could be a threat to him?"

"This is the only school Walter wished to attend," Lord Tootlington said. "He wanted to be challenged by its high standards. He came to be enrolled in no different way than the other boys. He earned it by achieving high marks at his previous schools. But once he was accepted, Sir John and I decided to break with standard policy and give him a room of his own. It would be safer for him as well as for any boy who would become his roommate."

"So, why did you change your mind?" I asked.

"After his first few weeks in Weatherby House, Walter telephoned me. He said he had met you on the day you were taking your entrance exams. He told me about your parents being killed at the World Trade Center. He knew Bulwick's roster was full, so he didn't think you could get in unless he gave up the second half of his room. Besides, he was uncomfortable being the only Shell to have such special attention. I suggested to Sir John that you be accepted into Bulwick School and to be Walter's roommate, providing, of course, that you met the academic requirements. In the meantime, I did a background check on your family. Somehow, our computers missed the IRA connection with your father and uncle. A gross oversight, to be sure, but one I am now glad to have happened, or I would never have captured Mr. Devlin."

I couldn't help but grin. "So, it wasn't Devlin who pulled the strings to get me in, it was you," I said.

Lord Tootlington returned my smile. "Blame Walter, if you must. It was his idea."

As the car rolled along, Lord Tootlington sat back in his seat. "When you sang the Connor Flanagan song that night, I sensed its power. If lyrics such as those could influence decent English citizens to turn so harshly upon a young Bulwick scholar, I wondered what effect they might have on a crowd of rough, Irish-born Rebels, people eager to resist British authority.

"When Walter came home last night and told me about your trouble with those gangsters, I remembered the song. I decided to come at once. This morning when you mentioned Pearse Devlin's name, my suspicions were confirmed. I also realized that with your help, I might be able to snare Devlin and put him away forever.

"I knew Devlin's arrest would incriminate your uncle and, consequently, the ruinous effect it would have upon you. I then recognized a possible solution. You could stay in England as my ward. Michael, it is important that I re-emphasize the peril you may encounter should you continue at Bulwick under my guardianship. Perhaps you will decide that terrorists have troubled your life too much already. You may wish to return to America, even under the condition of living in a foster-care facility."

The Rolls wended its way through Central London along wide avenues and tall buildings. Lord Tootlington took another call and talked for several minutes. While he did, I thought about the bullies I'd known: Joey Cardle, Billy Monmouth, Pearse Devlin, the Demons.

I remembered the good people: Mom and Dad, Felicity Brown, the Counts, Principal Brock, Tootles, Terrence, Alfred, Sir John, Mr. Epping, Oliver Hempstead, even Sir Starchface, Mr. Bassington. For every bully or terrorist, there are millions of people in every country, no matter what religion or political system it has, who want only to live peaceful lives and wish the same for others.

When Lord Tootlington put his phone back in his pocket, I said, "I don't need any more time to think about it. No matter where I go, there will always be bullies. I can only beat them by standing up to them. I can't live my life cowering under their threat. If it's all right with you, I'll take your offer right now."

"I had hoped you would feel that way," Lord Tootlington said, "but I insist you talk with Walter before making your decision final."

It was four in the afternoon when the limo pulled up to the curb at Weatherby House. Classes were over for the day. Lord Tootlington looked at me and said, "I will talk to you soon. Remember, whatever you decide, I will do everything I can to help you. Is there anything else?"

"Well, yeah, there is," I said. "Remember that girl I told you about, Felicity Brown?"

"The one who helped you get away from Devlin's men?" he asked.

"Right, her," I said. "Maybe you could look after her for a while. Devlin's guys know where she lives. They've got plenty reason to get back at her." I laughed remembering the roof shaft cover she'd dropped on their heads.

"I'll do that," Lord Tootlington said, "but those were Devlin's hired assassins. They were out to get you. When such men fail an assignment, they don't remain long to suffer its consequences."

"Maybe so," I said, "but it was my fault her house got trashed."

"I will see to that as well," he said.

"Thanks," I said. I began to reach for the door. "Oh, uh, there is just one other small favor."

"What's that?" he asked.

"Can I still call him Tootles?"

He looked at me with an impish grin. "I wish you would," he said. "That's what my friends called me when I was here."

I laughed. It was hard to picture the tall, stately Lord Tootlington as having the same nickname as my short, pudgy roommate.

At that, Lord Tootlington pressed a button, and the glass partition rolled down. "Please attend Mr. Hanlon's door," he said.

Instantly, it was opened. I stepped onto the sidewalk, waved to Lord Tootlington and ran up the stairs to my room.

Chapter Twenty-Six

Tootles was at his desk, staring at the door when I rushed in.

"I knew that was you," he said. "You're the only person who routinely charges down the hall like a deranged rhino."

As glad as I was to see him, I managed a hurt look. "Gee, and I thought you might like to know what your dad and I did today," I said with a sniff.

"All right," Tootles said eagerly. "What happened?"

"He took me to the zoo and gave me an ice cream."

"Oh, come on," Tootles said. "Okay, I really want to know."

"Well, first of all," I said, "I found out that your father is really *Lord* Tootlington."

Tootles looked up at me, a worried expression crossing his face. "Where'd you hear that?" he asked.

"It slipped out at Scotland Yard," I said. "Spends a fair amount of time there, I gather."

"Yes, I know," Tootles said. "So, what happened at Scotland Yard?"

I sat in the chair across from Tootles' desk. "Uncle Sean and Pearse Devlin were trying to skip the country," I said. "Thanks to Mr. Devlin, I've been a major contributor to some fake charity of his. He conned my uncle into giving most of the money I'd gotten after my parents were killed by terrorists, to a bunch of other terrorists. How's that for irony?"

"The IRA?" Tootles asked.

"A splinter group," I said. "My uncle didn't know it, but his friend wasn't working to help Ireland's Cause, only to steal my money. When Uncle figured that out, he told the police everything he knew. I feel sorry for him. He wanted so bad to be a hero like his brother, to do something for Ireland, that he ignored the fact that some of their leaders were nothing but mobsters. Turns out, besides ripping me off, Devlin wanted to kill your dad, and you too, if he could. Tricking me into singing the Connor Flanagan song was Devlin's way to flush your dad into the open. Kicker is, my father wrote that song. Can you believe it?"

Tootles stared blankly at me. "Your father wrote the song you sang at the talent show? When did he do that?"

"Twenty-five years ago during the Troubles," I said. "Dad was sixteen. Uncle Sean told me about it just this morning. He wrote it to stir his IRA pals into action."

"And a brilliant song it is," Tootles said. "I'm not surprised you were so taken by it. On the other hand, I'd have liked it a lot better if it hadn't been about the cold-blooded murder of one of my own ancestors. The villainous treachery of the plan is a part of the story your father left out of his song."

"What part is that?" I asked.

Tootles nodded, remembering the details. "Connor Flanagan, his father, friends and brothers, camped near Lord Tannahill's home that night. With the drawing of straws, Connor won the monstrous task of slaying Lord Tootlington in his sleep. At midnight, Connor broke in, sneaked through the manor's halls, and found my great-great-grandfather asleep in his chamber. He put a gun to his head and shot him.

"As it happened, a British army regiment was quartered in a field nearby. They heard the shot and went after the gunman. Very shortly, the soldiers trapped the Flanagan men at a place called Tannahill Bridge. Connor Flanagan, the youngest of the party, hid behind a rock. When the soldiers arrived, he opened fire.

He kept them at bay long enough to let his father and brothers slip across the bridge behind him. While Connor remained at the bridge, the others found cover on the other side. The Flanagans opened fire on the soldiers. During the exchange, Connor was shot, not through the heart with a British bullet, but in the back by one of his own men.

"Lord Tannahill's death left a little girl without a father," Tootles said. "Her name was Charlotte. Years later she married Phillip Tootlington, a neighboring lord's son. I am their great-great-grandson."

We stared at each other, Tootles and I, for almost a minute. I thought about everything he'd said.

"One of my family died that night, too," I said.

Tootles raised an eyebrow. "I suppose that means that you are a Flanagan."

"Yes," I said, "Connor Flanagan was my great-great-grand uncle. My father wrote that song during the height of the Troubles. As a kid, my dad was a rock-throwing, bomb-blasting, wild-eyed IRA fanatic. He also had a knack for writing protest songs. He sang his Connor Flanagan song just once. It did the job so well at rousing the IRA boys that one of them got up, ran into the street and shot the first British soldier he saw. The soldier got one round off, and the IRA guy was wounded. The RUC brought him in and found out about the song. Early the next morning they came for my father. Dad and Uncle Sean hadn't quite gotten home yet, but they watched it happen. The RUC thugs gunned down our whole family, everyone but Dad and Uncle Sean.

"Dad and Uncle hid out in Belfast for months. That's when my father met my mom. They were drawn to each other right away, love at first sight like people talk about. They knew that with her being Protestant and him Catholic they would always have a strained life anywhere they lived in Ireland. They decided to move away—somewhere that their mixed marriage would not matter. They scraped up enough money to book steerage class passage on a ship to New York.

"Dad and Mom became American citizens. They never looked back. Dad never again spoke out against the English. He never again gave a cent to the Irish Cause. Uncle Sean ran from Ireland too, but he landed in England, still holding to his old IRA ways. After 9/11 when Mom and Dad were killed by the al-Qaeda terrorists, I came here and you know all about that."

Tootles just stared. "That's some story," he said. "Since your uncle helped Pearse Devlin, won't he have to go to jail?"

"Yeah," I said. "Your dad doesn't think there's any way around it. He'll be in for a few years, at least."

"So, what's going to happen to you?" Tootles asked. "Uncle Sean's your only relative. Won't you have to go back to the United States?"

"Well, that's where it gets interesting," I said. "Your dad made me an offer. I can either go back to New York and live in foster care, or I can stay here at Bulwick School as his ward until I turn eighteen. He told me to think about both the good and the bad sides of each."

Tootles nodded. He knew what I was talking about, the dangers I would face if I stayed. "What did you say?" Tootles asked.

"He didn't want my answer right away," I said. "He wanted you to tell me what it was like walking around every day with a bull's-eye painted on your back."

"Right, that can be scary," Tootles said. He thought for a second. "I've had a few close calls."

"Anyway," I said, "I think you should have some say in the matter. It's one thing for us to be roommates, you know, go to classes, play rugby, those sorts of things. But what your dad is saying is that we'll be like brothers until we graduate. I'll be going places with your family, staying at your house. I'm thinking that you might like some space sometimes, some room to yourself, and you won't have it."

I stared at Tootles, waiting for a sign, something to let me know he got all this. He said nothing, so I went on. "See, you've got a tougher choice to make than I do, and I won't say yes until you think all that over. For me, it's either yes, and I stay here at Bulwick School, living like the son of a lord with all the privileges—and okay, some risks—that might go with that. Or I say no, go back to America and get put in a foster home. I've had classmates who were orphans or runaways or kids whose only living parent was in prison. That's who lives in places like that. From what I've seen, it's no picnic. So for me, it's a no-brainer. But for you? If you say yes, you're stuck with me. I could turn out to be a pain in the butt, and you wouldn't be able to get rid of me."

A smile crept over Tootles' face. "Oh, I understand, all right," he said, "and I'm beginning to dislike you already."

"There, see?" I said. "I knew you wouldn't take this seriously. But I really want you to think it through."

Tootles squeezed his eyes shut. He tapped his pudgy finger three times on his forehead, blinked, and then said, "Okay, I've thought it through. Where do I sign?"

I shook my head. "Oh, man," I said, "you still don't get it, do you?"

"No, *you* don't get it," Tootles said grinning. "This is the happiest day of my life. I'm calling Dad right now. From today on, we'll be brothers."

"Do you really mean that?" I said.

"I do," he said. "Look, since I was a little kid I've never had anybody I could really talk to. I've been in schools where most of the boys didn't have titles but knew that I did. They treated me like maybe I'd snitch on a bloke if he didn't bow down to me, like I was a spy or something. I hated every minute. And I've been in schools where many boys had titles. We had to treat each other like we were all best chums, even though we had nothing else in common. For once, with you, I've finally met someone who doesn't care who I am, what my family does, or any of that. And now it seems my father has made you an offer. You'll either go back to America and I'd never see you again, or you'll stay here at Bulwick School and be like my brother for the next five years. The choice seems to be all or nothing. Now, you're saying that I'm the one who gets to decide. All right, I'm going for all. Don't you see? You're the first real friend I've ever had."

I shook my head. "You're forgetting about Terrence and Alfred," I said.

"Yes, they're friends," Tootles said, "but I wonder, would they have stuck with me that day in September when Billy Monmouth pushed me to the ground?"

I thought about it. "Yeah, I think they would," I said.

"Well maybe, but they weren't there and you were," Tootles said. "And you were the one who got me through that Cromwell game. Not only got me through it, but saw to it that Oliver made me captain. I've never been good at any sport, but because of you I really feel part of the team."

"I've got to admit," I said. "When I first saw you, you were the last person I would have confused for a rugby player. But you've shown me you can't tell a book by its cover. The toughest guys at Bulwick School have knocked you down and you've bounced right up. Everyone says you're the heart and soul of our team."

Tootles laughed. "That might be a stretch," he said, "but don't you see? I've never tried so hard at anything in my life, and it's all because of you. You've taught me to believe in myself, and not just in the things I knew I could do, but other things as well. You're the first person I've ever really wanted to have for a friend. Maybe it's because you're an American. Americans don't have titles and all the baggage that goes with that. You couldn't care less if I was 'Tootles the Prince' or 'Tootles the Pauper.'"

"Is that why you looked so worried when I told you I knew

about your dad's title?"

"Yes," he said. "I was afraid you might change. But you haven't. You're the same as you were this morning, and I think you'll be the same after you take my father's offer. Which, if you don't, I'll haul you down to the yarder and give you a good thumping. Don't think I can't." At that, Tootles flexed his neck muscles as he had that day in September and then flashed a huge smile.

"All right," I said, "I guess you have thought it over."

"Yes, Brother, I have," he said. He held his hand out and we shook on it.

Epilogue

I wasn't about to test Tootles' threat, so I agreed to his father's offer. Tootles and I were roommates for our Shell and Remove years. Then, for three years, we had rooms next to each other on Weatherby's second floor. We were never more than a knock on the wall away if either of us needed something, and only a few doors from Alfred and Terrence. Another thing: I never once woke them up with a screamer. Although I thought about my parents a lot, especially my dad, my nightmares were over. I visited my uncle often, and over time he understood my father's refusal to aid the IRA.

There was something else that Tootles, Terrence, Alfred, and I learned from each other: Titles and wealth don't matter much when it comes to living a happy and rewarding life. We set high goals for ourselves and found ways to pull them off. And it didn't matter whether we were British lords, African scholars, or American orphans.

Lord Tootlington kept his word and paid for my whole time at Bulwick School. He also saw to it that Felicity Brown's apartment was put back into shape. He even arranged for her mom to get some really good medical care and her dad to get a decent job. With that done, Felicity concentrated on her classes. She flew through them, getting top marks, and making a strong case for getting into college, which she did.

Every month or so, Bulwick School held dance parties with the girls' schools. I think Tootles talked Sir John into allowing top students to invite their own dates as a reward for good grades. I didn't need any more incentive than that. Felicity Brown became my partner for every dance for the next four-and-a-half years, with every Bulwick boy looking at me like I was the luckiest guy in all of England.

When I turned eighteen in September of my last year, the one trust fund that Pearse Devlin hadn't stolen was worth a lot, but not enough for any college in the United Kingdom. I applied for scholarships in the United States and got a full ride at Columbia University in Manhattan, not far from where the World Trade Center once stood. I took it gladly and decided to study international relations.

Tootles, Terrence, and Alfred each got into Oxford, and I starting packing for New York. Uncle Sean got out of prison in time for my Bulwick School graduation. He came, but I could tell he felt out of place in front of so many people who knew where he'd been for the past five years.

I got an apartment in Manhattan and talked Uncle Sean into coming with me. We both knew if he stayed in England, his old IRA buddies would do him more harm than good. So we packed, and with Felicity between us, had one last night of music and ham sandwiches at Casey's.

The next morning Uncle and I flew to New York. On my first day home I grabbed a taxi and went to Ground Zero. It still showed the awful scars of that day in 2001 that changed the world. Standing there, I thought about how Mom and Dad had met in Belfast, why they came to America, and how they had died—all because of terrorists.

I started my first year at Columbia with only one regret—I would be an ocean away from Felicity Brown while she studied medicine in London.

Lord Tootlington helped me there, too. He found a summer job for me working in London for the US embassy, which was less than three blocks from Felicity's school. So that's where I spent my college breaks. All the while she and I were making more permanent plans for after graduation.

Not long after leaving Bulwick School, Tootles thinned out and lost his chubby, choirboy appearance. He shot up about eight inches and looks more like his dad now than his mom. Two years ago he married a Wycombe Abbey girl and now they have a son whom they've named Michael in my honor. One day, Tootles tells me, he will apply for his father's Anti-Terrorist seat in the House of Lords. I know he'll keep his great sense of humor, but with his position in Parliament his worries will be many. Still, I know there isn't a terrorist in the world who can break his spirit.

For my part, I finished my undergrad courses at Columbia and went on to George Washington University for a degree in law. On the same day, Felicity graduated from the Royal College of Surgeons as a doctor in pediatrics. We were married last year and she is now just three months from delivering our first child, a son. His name will be Walter Tootlington Hanlon, and he will go through his entire life trying to explain to his friends why his parents call him Tootles.

One day, I'll run for office and use what I've learned to work for world peace. My hope is that Tootles and I will team up and take on any bully or terrorist who comes our way. And the world will be a happier place for it.

The End

About Robert A. Lytle

I was born in 1944 and grew up with my parents and three older sisters on Mackinaw Street in Saginaw, Michigan. My father, a high school agriculture teacher, was an avid outdoorsman as well as a self-taught poet. From him I learned to fish, hunt and play a variety of sports. Also, by his example, I wrote stories and poems as a way to express my interest in those activities.

When I was five years old, our family inherited a crude but habitable cabin in the Les Cheneaux Islands of Michigan's Upper Peninsula. I spent my next thirteen summers fishing, swimming, and hiking. Even rainy days were filled with indoor games, reading, and socializing.

As college approached, I knew my carefree summers were over. I had to earn my way. Mackinac Island, with all its hotels and other employment opportunities, was only a hop, skip, and a boat ride from my beloved family summer cabin. I landed a job as a hotel dock porter for one summer, and then three more assisting boaters on the island's yacht dock. The dream lived on.

I took my fourth year of pharmacy school at Queen's University in Belfast, Northern Ireland where I played basketball, guitar, and studied, in about that order. It was 1966-67—the very early stages of the Troubles.

I returned home for my final "Mackinac" summer at the marina, and there, I met my future wife.

Graduation, marriage, a "real" job as pharmacist, and the beginning of our new family, which was to grow to four sons, called me away from northern Michigan for nearly twenty-five years.

During that time I bought an old-fashioned, corner drugstore in downtown Rochester, Michigan, as well as a house a few blocks away. That's where we made our home for the next thirty-five years. For each of my boys I wrote songs and poems. I kept them in a folder, which became like a picture book—a way to remember their childhood days.

As a drugstore owner, I wrote my own ads and was encouraged to write a self-help medical advice book. I did, but the man who prompted me to write it and would be its promoter, passed away as the book was being printed. Three thousand books sat, virtually unsalable, in the store's basement. It was a financial flop.

I did, however, learn that I loved the whole writing process—from researching each subject to revising until it reached a polished, final form. I decided to try my hand at a novel. "Write what you know about," is the mantra authors are told to follow, so I decided to explore my Northern Michigan experiences and embellish them into a story. Three years and hundreds of rejections later *Mackinac Passage: A Summer Adventure* was published by a Michigan publisher. Two more Mackinac stories quickly followed. Then, by a simple extension into Rochester lore, I came to write the time-travel adventure, *Three Rivers Crossing*, published in 2000. A fourth Mackinac story, *The Mystery at Round Island*

Light, followed in 2001.

In 2000 I became involved with the Rochester Grangers, a vintage baseball club. Ballists, as we are called, dress in period uniforms and compete with other clubs from around the Midwest. We play by the gentlemanly rules of the 1850s and '60s—no gloves, spitting, cursing, or sliding. Baseball, the Civil War, and life in a northern state at that time became the subjects of my next novel, *A Pitch in Time*. Published in December 2002, it was runner-up for the prestigious Ben Franklin Award.

A fifth Mackinac Passage story, *Pirate Party*, featuring the 1812 attack by the British forces upon Fort Mackinac, was published in 2005.

Mr. Blair's Labyrinth, a time-travel, Great Depression-era story featuring my historic home, one of its gardens, and two of my grandsons, was published in 2011.

When not actively writing or working in my store, I visit schools and organizations to discuss a variety of subjects, including writing, history, music, and medicine.

CPSIA information can be obtained
at www.ICGtesting.com
Printed in the USA
FFOW03n2144190617
36825FF